FIREFLY

TIRTHA. C

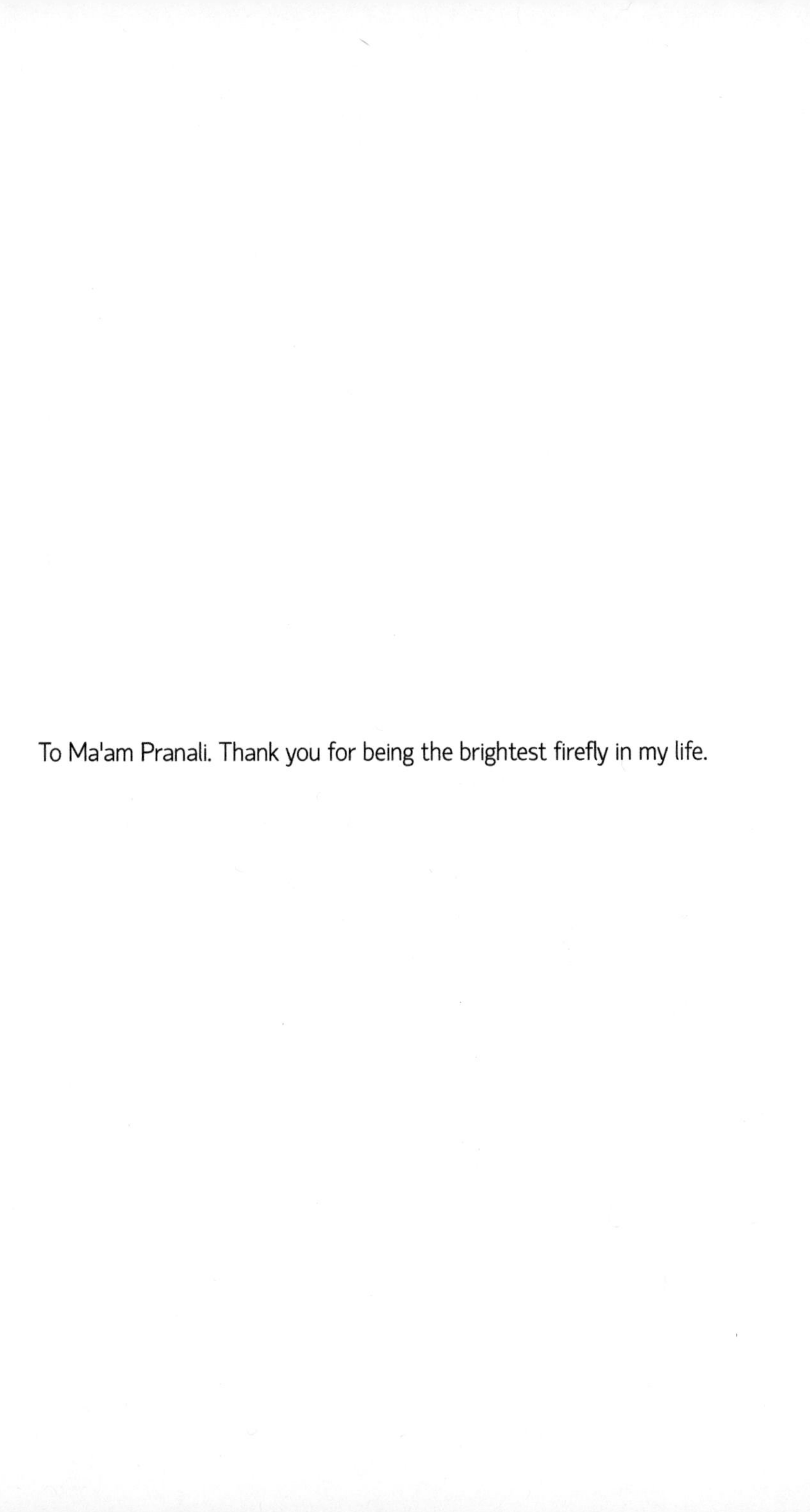

To Ma'am Pranali. Thank you for being the brightest firefly in my life.

Contents

Acknowledgements

Thank you Notion Press Publications for helping me as always. Special thanks to Anjali Jadhav for guiding me and solving all my difficulties.

CHAPTER ONE

Chapter 1

Amelia Araste picked her suitcase from the taxi trunk and bought it down with a thud. The Hamlington air had the fragrance of both excitement and nervous. She paid the driver, with a tip, a thing she saw a lady doing before and hung her bag on the shoulders and pulled the suitcase behind her. Students were standing in small groups and everyone was struggling to fit in the new environment. Amelia saw a girl in an oversized shirt, who was struggling with her bags. The girl had two bags and a large suitcase with her. She walked up to some people but within a few seconds she returned with a sad expression on her face. Amelia put on a big smile on her face and approached her. "I am Amelia Araste. Do you wanna hang out together?" The girl looked at her and Amelia felt as if she saw tears in her eyes. "I am Jessica Marues. I would love to hang out with you Amelia." Amelia smiled, showing her aligned, bright and perfect teeth. She pulled out a band from her pocket and tied her long red hair in a bun. Her blue eyes sparkled as her rosy cheeks with freckles glowed as she held Jessica's plump hand, "Let's find more friends." Jessica nodded her head as she trotted happily behind Amelia, still struggling with her luggage.

"I am Tanya. Fr...fr...from Galfred. I...have dysarthria....I want....to...j...j...jo...join your.....g...g...g...g...gr..group..." "Get going from here. We do need another person in our group but it surely won't be you and that's for sure." "Why can't she join your group? Don't mind me, I happen to be curious." The girls turned towards Amelia. "I will explain it in a simple sentence, red head. People like her can't be with us. She is a pushover. Now, excuse us," the group of 6 walked away from leaving behind a gloomy Tanya. "Come with us. We are lacking a member." Amelia put her hand on her shoulder which made Tanya's face smile. She looked at the girls standing behind Amelia. A fat girl, a girl with extreme dark complexion, a girl with her hair cut short as a boy and two girls dressed like old aunts. "Sure."

The group sat on the nearest table. The girl with a boy cut asked, "Would anyone try and explain why everyone is making groups?" "It was written on the admission letter that we have the freedom to choose 7 roommates. Of course, people are trying to find and make group of people with same preferences and taste as them as that helps them to get along pretty well," Jessica spoke up. "Shouldn't we start with our introductions, hobbies and do mention your majors too." "Yeah, let's do it group leader!" Amelia laughed at this remark. "No need to put me in charge. I am not going to lead anyone and nor is anyone else going to do it. Let's have a friendly vibe among us." The girls smiled at this suggestion. Everyone was rejected from some or the other group by their 'Group Leaders'. "I am Amelia from the countryside of Hamlington. My hobbies include playing sports and reading. My major is fashion designing." "I am Jessica from Harlend. I love to paint and dance. My major is arts." "I....am Tanya...fr...fr... from Galfred. I...l... like to...s....si... sing. My....m....m....m...ma....major is....c.....che....chem.....chemi....chemistry." "I am Fiona and this is my twin sister Maria from Hamlington. We both excel in mimicking other people and have fun in this way. We are also majoring in arts." "I am Yaniya from Hamlington and I like playing drums. My major is music." "I am Georgia from Hamlington. I love to cook. My major is also arts."

Amelia took out chocolates from her bag and kept them on the table, "I made these before coming here. Can you try and tell me whether they taste good?" The girls looked at each other and shyly each of them took the chocolates one by one. Amelia smiled as each girl ate the chocolates and had a big smile on their face. "It is really yummy." "Yes, we also agree." "Ye..yes." "I will make more from now on. We could eat it all the time" Amelia smiled and the others also showed their happiness by smiling brightly. "The dorm inspector is here. Let's go!" Everyone got up as soon Fiona said this. Amelia saw that her group was already helping each other to carry the extra bags. 'I found friends' she smiled to herself.

Room 201. Tanya opened the door. The girls struggled to dump the suitcases inside. Seven girls with fifteen huge suitcases. Two big and spacious rooms, one of them was painted in cream with a huge table with seven chairs that was supposed to serve as the study table. The room also had a sofa, with a window above it, directly opposite of the door where they were currently standing. The bathroom was on the left side. The girls then moved to the next room that was painted in turquoise. "Let's start choosing our beds and then we could decorate the room," Amelia suggested. Tanya had closed the door. "I...h...ha...have an...i...i...idea. Why........ don't....w...ww... we draw lots....t....t....t....tt.... to select....ea...eac... each of our.......b.....b.....b....b....beds?"

Jessica clapped her hands with excitement. The twins squealed with joy. Amelia looked around her. They were 19 years old but their hearts seemed like a five year old." 'When people don't express their emotions occasionally, they pile up and childish things like these help them to express those small pieces of joy, anger, frustration or sorrow.'

Seven beds; each had a new neighbor beside them. Three on the right, three on the left and one bed seemed as the head of all the beds. It wasn't the slightest surprise when the head bed's was acclaimed by Amelia's luck. "Believe it or not, you are the leader of our group!" Georgia exclaimed. Amelia laughed this remark off. Yaniya, Georgia and Fiona got their beds on the left side and Maria, Jessica and Tanya were on the right. There were 3 closets opposite the head bed. The girls took out their stuff on their beds. "Anyone has speaker with them?" Amelia asked the girls. Yaniya took out hers and gave it to Amelia. Within minutes, the voice of Justin Bieber echoed in their room. "Anyone interested in making a playlist together. All the hands went in the air.

Dancing on the tunes of vivid songs of Justin Bieber, Taylor Swift, Anne Maria, BTS, Sean Paul, Dua Lipa and various other artists, the girls cleaned the dirty rooms and dusted all the furniture. They had named their playlist Copines which translated as friends in French. Within an hour, along with all the dusting even the mopping was completed without any fuss. Some people outside were arguing outside in the corridors of the dorm. Maybe it was that some girls didn't want to do any work, while some didn't like to be ordered around. Whatever the reason was, this group of seven was pretty co-ordinated. "Got paints?" Amelia looked at the others with puppy eyes that made everyone laugh. Soon everyone was painting something or other on the walls. "This makes me feel more at home," Georgia smiled. Amelia quietly took out a giant, white dream catcher from her bag and hung it to the window of their study room. She turned at the others who were smiling seeing her tie it up, "All our bad dreams will now be discarded."

"Phew, don't you think we left some space where we could've painted a little more?" "No Jessica. I don't think I can paint for some hours now. I wonder whether I can eat anything with these tired hands." Tanya laughed at Yaniya, "I...wi...wi...will feed...yo..you...Yaniya. I......promise." Yaniya smiled heartily and blew a kiss towards Tanya. "It's 7PM now. Let's take turns to wash up. The cafeteria starts at 7:30PM. We can make it till 8PM." Jessica nodded as Amelia suggested it.

The cafeteria was lit up beautifully. All the students were talking loudly. Some boys were chasing each other while some girls were pampering each other. Some couples were sitting together while eating and talking lovingly. Amelia scanned the area with his eyes. "The counter is there. We need to make our cards there." They walked towards the counter. Another group of boys were standing ahead of them, making their cards. "E...exc....excuse...m...m...me, can you tell h...ho....ho......ho...how long it takessssss....t....t....t...to make a c......c.....ca....card?" "3 minutes stutter." "Too rude," Yaniya commented loud. "Saying what's the truth doesn't make you any wrong," the guy turned and looked Yaniya dead in the eye, "right, DUDE?" Amelia held the angry Yaniya's hand. "Let's not make a problem here, shall we?" Amelia glared angrily at the guy. "Sure shabby," the guy smirked as he turned his back towards them.

The girls were wearing ordinary dresses that seemed extremely dull and boring. “Guys look out for girls that are prettily dressed, right?” Jessica looked down her loose PJs and oversized shirt. “We are not here to please any guy” Amelia stated loudly looking at the other girls that wear smirking at their bad fashion sense. Amelia was herself dressed shabbily. Her long, straight red hair, tied in a messy bun and she was wearing her reading glasses. She hadn’t put on any make up, just like her roommates. This girl squad was totally different than the rest of the girls. The rest of the girl students were dressed prettily. After the guys were done with their card process, Amelia and her friends stepped forward. Within some time, with cards in their hands, the girls went to get their dinner. They spotted an empty table, in the corner of the hall. They sat down and started eating their food. “What is the exact length of your hair Georgia?” Maria turned towards Georgia as she gulped the food down her throat. “If I let them open, they reach to my knees.” Everyone widened their eyes. Georgia also had made a bun since morning. “T....t.....th....th.....that’s i...i...imp....impressive!” Georgia blushed at Tanya’s remark. “Thanks.” “Amelia’s hair colour is the rarest. I haven’t seen red hair before. Even here, you can see people with ginger hair but your hair are particularly tomato red.” Amelia smiled despite of having her whole mouth filled with food that enlarged her cheeks. The girls laughed at her as Amelia too joined in.

Amelia was laughing as her eyes again wandered around. The other girls on the tables around them were looking at these girls with peculiar disgust. Amelia shook her head as she joined the group conversation about different pets. Time passed while laughing and this seemed to deepen the bond between the girls. “What should we call our group?”

"Shabby sounds better for y'all" a high pitched voice said. A girl from the table beside them spoke up. Amelia smiled at her, "You should have approached us first if you were interested in joining our group. You shouldn't be shy." The girl smirked as she raised an eyebrow at Amelia, "Who wants to join you? You are just a bunch of weaklings. Uh Huh wait...I couldn't call this girl a WEAKLING." The girl pointed her finger straight at Jessica, who seemed embarrassed as the others laughed at her. "It's a first time in my life, seeing a jerk introducing herself," Amelia scowled at the girl. The girl gasped as she was taken aback. "Let's get back to the dorm before things get ugly" Maria suggested. Fiona looked around and saw that people from the other tables were slowly turning their attention towards them. Amelia nodded and the girls started towards the counter to return their plates. Amelia was the last in the line. She smiled politely at the girl who was pissing them earlier. That seemed to anger the girl even a lot more. Amelia passed her table and gave her plate to the counter. Jessica, Fiona, Maria, Tanya and Georgia were already on their way out. Yaniya was beside Amelia, talking about the various instruments she had tried playing before she had started playing drums. Yaniya was the first one to see the girl approaching them in anger. "Do you think that you own this place?" Amelia rolled her eyes, "I thought we had finished this conversation earlier. Why don't you get the hint that we are not interested in wasting our time on you?' The girl smirked at her, "I won't let you get off with this. I hope you keep that in your mind." Amelia smiled and nodded.

Sometimes, it's just your smile and cool head that makes people hate you. Yaniya started walking away from this drama and Amelia turned to join her, when all of her sudden, the girl pulled Amelia's hair and brutally. Amelia shrieked as the attention of all the students turned towards this commotion. Yaniya rushed as fast as she could while the other girls stood where they were; beside the door. Amelia was clearly in pain but she signaled Yaniya not to intervene. She bought her left leg swiftly and kicked the girl's leg with force. The girl hadn't seen this coming and she fell instantly and Amelia fell forward as she was released from the grip. A boy quickly caught Amelia in time; if not, then Amelia would have had a nosebleed for sure. The bun that had tied her fiery red hair was open and her hair locks were decorating her face beautifully. Amelia looked at the owner of the hand that held her arm. The boy had a fair complexion with brown hair that were beautifully messy and beautiful blue eyes that spoke the language of the ocean. He pulled her with a strong pull and Amelia found herself against his firm chest. She mumbled a 'thank you' and walked towards the exit. The girl behind was howling with pain. Yaniya followed Amelia closely as they joined the others outside the cafeteria.

The girls breathed normally when they were way too far from the cafeteria. Everyone turned towards Amelia. She was red from the embarrassment. Jessica placed her hand on Amelia's shoulder. Amelia looked at her and smiled. The others seemed a bit surprised seeing her smile. "Well let's consider this the beginning of our college life. It wasn't that bad and the best thing, I didn't have any locks pulled off. Imagine, my first day and I will be roaming bald. Gosh! I don't even wanna imagine that," Amelia burst out laughing with the others. "Let's get going, we have our first day tomorrow."

Back in the cafeteria, the girl got up and dusted her skirt. She looked at the onlookers, "Go and eat your stuff!

Is this some kind of period drama going on? And you..." she turned to the boy who had helped Amelia, "You really wanted to help the girl that insulted your cousin? What's gone into you Aiden?" "Ashley, you started it all first. She wasn't sticking her nose where it didn't belong. You had no right to insult anyone like that, so you should better ask yourself why I didn't stand for you because I believe I gave you enough reasons to know it better now. I got to be going now. I hope you don't waste your first year by getting in such things or else you know that uncle is just a call away." Aiden walked away leaving Ashley speechless. Ashley's gang came up to her, "Are you okay?" Ashley glared at them angrily and they shut their mouths for any further questions. 'That red head is going to regret crossing me.'

Far from this scene, a guy smirked as he ran up to Aiden, "Quite a beauty there!" "Ashley?" "Ashley's not the one I am talking about." Aiden smiled as the boy continued, "The red head is quite a beauty that's hard to miss anyone's eyes." "Totally agreeable Noah but we don't know anything about her." "Yet." Aiden laughed at his best friend as they both raced their way to their dorm.

AMELIA'S DIARY:

I made friends, just like I have always wanted. I genuinely and happily accept God's plan for me but now I feel like for sometime, only for few moment and some years, I should be selfish. I broke up from my past life and now I don't want to be trapped by those things that I don't even want to remember. The people are really warm and cheerful here and they acknowledge me with love and care. I thought that in big cities, people don't judge and are friendly but we were judged on the basis of our clothing during dinner. We worked hard the entire day and decorated our room while the others pampered themselves. The cafeteria was crowded with people with people dressed richly. Why do people dress so much when they have to eat and sleep after a tiring day? We went down in our comfortable clothes afterall the only reason behind wearing clothes is covering the body while providing comfort. And on top of that I fought with another girl but I will try to mend this little fight and turn her into my friend. I was locked in my life and problems from a long time but I know one thing, I will not ponder over the past. The future holds many opportunities and I will cherish everything I can until the autumn of my life comes.

CHAPTER TWO

Chapter 2

"Maria, wear the black skirt beneath the cream blouse and Fiona white would suit better on the brown skirt" Amelia instructed the twins. Last night after the scene, the girls came and put off the lights of their room. Amelia sat up and looked at the girls who wearing lying on their beds, "Let's change our outfits tomorrow." The girls, who had just closed their eyes and were pretending to sleep, sat up and looked at the head bed. "I am in" Yaniya and Georgia responded quickly. The twins nodded their heads, "We also want a change from our old clothing set. We look like our old aunt Tessie, we smell like our old aunt Tessie." Everyone laughed at this old line of Ron Weasley from the Harry Potter. Jessica smiled, "I guess that's just what I need." "Meeee......tooo...I a...am...in." "So, let's sleep tight, we have a long day tomorrow."

They were all up at 7AM. Jessica knew how to style one's hair, Yaniya and Tanya were both engaged in cutting some of the clothing while Georgia and the twins were stitching the bits as instructed by Amelia, who was overlooking all the progress and was pairing everyone's dresses. The classes started at 11AM and thus they had a lot of time. "Fiona go and take your bath, I have selected your dress. Call me after you are done. I will hand your clothes in."

Fiona rushed as Amelia set her dress aside. "Nice idea" Yaniya had come up to Amelia without her noticing it. "Thanks and thank you for helping me too." "I know why you did this" Yaniya whispered. Amelia turned at Yaniya and looked her dead in her eye as she came down to her ear, "It was a suggestion" and smiled brightly.

Yaniya felt confused as Amelia walked away from her. 'She did this to lift up everyone's mood. However, she doesn't like sympathy or gratefulness. It's just like she doesn't want herself be acknowledged and appreciated by all or is it because something happened to her in the past?' Yaniya looked at Amelia as she was smiling and laughing while talking with the others. "Amelia please hand my dress." Georgia had finished her bath. The rest were applying their makeup and styling their hairs. Amelia handed Georgia her clothes and looked at her watch. "We have still an hour. I am going to have bath. Tanya, will you hand me my clothes?" Tanya smiled and nodded. She was wearing a red blouse and leather skirt. It showed her hourglass figure beautifully and she loved the outfit at the first sight. Jessica had tied Tanya's hair in a low bun. Tanya had asked Amelia whether she could select a dress for her and Amelia had agreed to it. She wanted to repay Amelia's kindness by selecting a perfect outfit for her. After five minutes, Tanya smiled at her choice. Amelia was going to look the most beautiful girl in the entire campus and she was sure of it.

Tanya looked around at the buzzing going on around her. Everyone was looking beautifully dressed up. Fiona had tied her hair in a long ponytail and was wearing a sparkling white shirt with long arms and a coffee brown skirt that went from her waist to half an inch above her knee. Beneath that she was wearing black long socks and black shoes. Her twin Maria wore a cream turtleneck blouse and a short black skirt with short socks and white shoes. She had left her hair open. 'Amelia kept their dresses and styles completely opposite emphasizing that although they are twins, their personalities differ a lot' Tanya thought. Yaniya was brushing her short, black hair. She looked like a boy with her hairstyle and her fashion was matching her aura very well. She was wearing blue hot pant and black blouse with very thin strips on the either side. An oversized checked shirt of the colours of red and black (which clearly belonged to Jessica) was acting as her jacket. Jessica was happily smiling at her outfit. She was wearing a black turtleneck top with black pants and a cream long overcoat to match and white sneakers and her hair were tied into a bun. Georgia had just put on her last piece of clothing. She was wearing distressed jeans and a dark brown tank top. Her belly button was visible and she had one of Jessica's checked shirts which had the combination of cream and brown colour with her curly hair let loose.

"Tanya hand me my clothes." Tanya trotted happily and gave Amelia her clothes. She sat applying makeup on everyone's face. Within some minutes, as Tanya had finished applying makeup for everyone, Amelia emerged out of the bathroom. All turned their heads in her direction. Amelia was wearing a pistachio green tank top and a white shrug, which showed her perfect jaw line and her beautiful collarbones. Beneath that she had a mini checked skirt with the colour combinations of white and light pistachio green. She wore small white socks and a beautiful pair of white shoes. "Thank you Tanya, this is the most amazing dress I have ever worn." "Yo.....y....you look.....r....re...re.....re.....re....really beautiful. I didn't im....im......i....i.....imagine t..ttt.....ttt...that you w....w...wou.....woul.......would look th........this pr.....pr.....prr......pretty in th...th....th....this dress. I a....m.....am glad I c...co...cou.....cou.....could he......e.......he.....help." Amelia nodded her head and smiled as she went to Jessica. "Style mine now." Jessica grinned as she opened Amelia's bun. Her red locks bounced their way down to her shoulder. She brushed her with the comb and left it open. "Just like that?" Amelia looked with puppy eyes, expecting Jessica's answer. Jessica laughed, "No need to do more. Your hair doesn't need to be styled today. They are the prettiest I have ever seen and they make your face look even more beautiful. They are wavy and beautiful. I am not going to tie them up."Amelia blushed, "Thanks." Georgia came and applied a little bit of blush of Amelia's cheek. "You're all done." Amelia smiled, "We look amazing. Let's take a photo." Yaniya took out her selfie stick and CLICK, CLICK, CLICK.

"Aiden did you see the red head yet?" Aiden shook his head "Could we just stop talking about her? She is not that special." Deep in his heart, he knew that he too wanted to see the girl from last night but he didn't want to be obvious about his feelings to Noah. She was brave and didn't give in to Ashley's bullying. His cousin was spoilt, selfish, a desperate attention seeker. He pretended not to know Ashley and didn't tell anyone that she was his cousin; anyone didn't include Noah. Noah knew about Ashley and Aiden's relation but as an outsider to his family, he knew he would be safe to stay away from the family. "We are seniors this year Aiden and we won't be playing basketball with our buddies after this year. We need to play every chance we get." "I think the match is day after tomorrow. Wanna practice this evening after the classes? I think I should play more to exercise my body." "Sure man, let me call the others and tell them that A&N are in the team again. You won't believe how happy..." Noah stopped suddenly making Aiden look in the direction he was looking in.

All the people in the corridor had their eyes fixed on Amelia's squad. Noah saw 'red head' looking as a royal princess with her escorts, three on either of her sides. Aiden was mesmerized by Amelia as the girls walked past the open jaws to their lockers. Far in the corner, Ashley bit her lip out of anger, seeing that all the attention was focused on the girl who had embarrassed her the other day. She pulled something from her purse and fixed it between her fingers of the inner palm. She walked up to Amelia who was talking to Tanya and Georgia as they were on their way to the class. "Hey" Ashley smiled at them. Aiden, who was also on his way Amelia to introduce himself formally, but stopped in his tracks, seeing what his cousin was up to. "I am so sorry for yesterday, I shouldn't have said anything like that to hurt you guys, I am so sorry." Amelia gave her cheerful smile and placed her hand on Ashley's shoulder, "It's fine." "So friends?" Ashley stuck her hand out. Amelia nodded her head and held Ashley's hand when she felt a piercing pain through her palm. Ashley tightened her grip and shook Amelia's hand firmly. It was Noah and then the others who saw blood dropping from between their palms. He was closer to Amelia, so he ran and pushed Ashley with such a force that Ashley fell hard on the ground. Amelia was astonishing quite. Aiden had rushed behind Noah and he held Amelia's hand. A big needle was stuck deep in her palm. Noah took one glance at her hand and yelled at Ashley, "Do you think this thing is cool? Let me take you to the dean." "Are you my mom? Get lost from here. She deserved it. Now, excuse me." Noah glared angrily at the disappearing figure of Ashley. "Let's go to the infirmary.

Noah, cover up for me and someone from her major kindly cover up for her." Aiden and Amelia walked from the locker room towards the infirmary. There was a corridor between the locker room and the infirmary. "You are really strong. You didn't show any signs of pain. Are you okay or in shock?" Amelia smiled at this question, "I am fine, it's just a needle. I will probably a shot at worse." Aiden smiled in confusion, "My name is Aiden Hourste." "Amelia Araste."

"Just a little more pain young lady. The needle is very deep now. Who plays with needles nowadays?" Aiden looked at the expressionless Amelia who was sitting on a bed. Her face didn't show any pain but Aiden was observing her hand. She was clutching the pillow tightly. The nurse pulled the remaining part of the needle swiftly, that caused her more pain as her buried her nails deep in the pillow. The needle had blocked the path of the blood and with it being removed, the blood oozed out. The nurse applied ointment after cleaning the blood with cotton and bandaged her hand. She then took out a bacteria killing bottle and filled the liquid in an injection. "Remove your shrug." She applied a disinfecting liquid to cleanse the area and gave her the shot. Amelia sat there as it were nothing and Aiden was quite confused at her actions. Normally girls, shriek and scream or at least complain about the pain but here was a girl who wasn't allowing any word of pain escape her lips. Amelia put her shrug on and thanked the nurse. "Don't forget to clean your wound in every six hours and bandage it properly." "I won't forget it." Aiden thanked the nurse and ran after the speeding Amelia. "That's the second time I got your back." Confusion flooded over Amelia's face. "Yesterday night at the cafeteria," Aiden reminded her and Amelia allowed herself to smile. The sun was shining on them. "We are already late and the lectures might be already halfway so there is no point in going. Wanna hang out?" "Why not?"

"So you are from the countryside? It doesn't look like that though." "Appearances are deceptive." Aiden laughed and Amelia stared at the guy in front of her. He wasn't anything like her. She belonged to a poor family and had spent her life in a small house that didn't even have a privileged of sunlight. This guy in front of her, was majoring in Medicine, came from a wealthy household, had girls sneaking and taking peeps of him and still was down to earth. She was using this chance to start over her life once again and everyone loved to spend their time with her. She considered it as a blessing that she had met a lot of lovely people. She was thinking about these things, when Aiden caught her staring at him. Amelia looked away from his eyes as she felt her cheeks burning red, "The countryside is beautiful." "Well, that M'lady I can sense that from you." Aiden and Amelia turned to look at this intruder. Noah was grinning sheepishly at them and behind him, Amelia's roommates were standing and waving their hands at them. "Can...." "Yeah let them join us."

"These are my roommates, Jessica, Georgia, Fiona, Maria, Yaniya and Tanya."Aiden and Noah smiled and shook all their hands. "Noah, my best friend and a woman charmer," Noah extended his hand out to Amelia but pulled it back when he saw the bandage. "Our handshake is still pending." "Let my hand heal, we will have our mini handshake ceremony. All hands can attend it." Everyone burst out laughing. Noah whispered to Aiden, "She is really good" to which Aiden smirked. The group spoke for some time about the various courses and part time jobs available. After a short while, Aiden stood up and gathered his coat. "We have our class now and now that I have missed my first class, it would only be appropriate for me to not miss the others. Class president setting bad example for others, well I don't like the sound of that. I will text you later, until next time." Aiden waved and technically dragged Noah from the crowd. "Do you like him?" Yaniya asked the smiling Amelia. Jessica grinned, "Look at her blushing so happily." Without waiting for Amelia's reply, Tanya continued, "Isn't h.....h....h....he th.....the one wh...wh....wh....who s....a...sa........ed...saved you yest...yester.....yesterday too?" Amelia nodded, "Yes..." "He seems so fine. God I am so jealous right now," Georgia laughed. Fiona and Maria tapped Amelia on her head as all the friends were laughing and teasing Amelia. Amelia bought herself to control, "Our second class starts now. We need to be going." The girls stopped giggling but started again when Yaniya said, "She didn't say no." Amelia hit Yaniya with her left hand as she struggled not to show her red face. Amelia's phone rang and her face turned pale. She ignored the call, looked up and smiled, "You guys get going; I will join you in the class." As soon as they were out of sight, Amelia dialed the number, "I thought I told you that I won't be picking any of your calls. What is it this time?"

"Well Professor Hayle was very friendly but why do I think it was because it was our first day. What do you all think?" "Fiona, you are not wrong. I think he wanted to seem approachable and friendly, he might not be exactly that way." "I guess we all agree to that Jessica, but did you see Amelia's pale face when she received the call?" Georgia asked this question and the professor walked in. The professor started with the basic introductions. The conversation was ended without reaching a result and was forgotten as the class continued further without any obstacle.

"Got an injury already cowgirl," Ashley and her minions had come to Amelia and her friends when they were helping some seniors to hand a banner. The university had only two classes for all the students on the first day as they had a fresher's party on the first day. The whole campus was buzzing with excitement for their first party. "You lost that chance to become friends with us. Talk about missing opportunities." "You think that I need friends, like you? My squad has an actual fashion taste, not like yours that want to impress people with some thrift store ideas and you might have no idea that the fresher's party needs a partner, got any date?"

"My friends don't need any advice or instruction from you because anything you can do perfectly is just demotivate others and it's not a compulsion to bring a partner with you. The notice regarding instructions is pinned exactly at your right." "Ashley, back off and do the work that is assigned for you." "Noah? Hey." "Hey Amelia, hey girls," the girls smiled and grinned as they had already named Aiden and Noah as their 'knights in shining armor.' "Dear senior, why do you interfere between us? Why do you differentiate among us?" "You called your roommates 'Squad' while Amelia used the term 'Friends'. You should learn something from her. Now, I guess you are required there. Lots of balloons need to be blown. Take your squad. Before going, let me tell you that Amelia has company tonight." "Who is taking this loser? Has he lost his screws?" Amelia turned towards Noah with a puzzling look. "Me."

AMELIA'S DIARY:

Jealousy and self obsession can destroy any person within minutes. My handwriting might suck but what else can you expect from a girl who got a needle stuck in her palm and then treated it? My friends and I dressed up prettily but the girl who I fought with yesterday night (her name is Ashley) lost her chance to be my friend and I want to avoid her as much as I can. People who judge others on their life choices or the way they dress or the brand they are wearing are of the low kind. God didn't made anyone perfect but some people assume that they are PERFECT and have the authority to say and do as they please, not knowing that it might hurt someone and destroy their confidence. In my hometown, I never had friends, so this face of the society is new to me and even I am learning new things and these things show the harsh reality of the world. He called me again. I thought I was free here but my past keeps dragging me down. He says he is hurt by my decision of leaving him and coming here to live. Talking about being hurt, I am over it. I can't be hurt more, neither mentality nor physically. I am used to pain, so these little gestures and little hate words cannot destroy me because I am already destroyed. I only had a fake smile plastered to this face but after making friend, maybe my heart will learn to smile too. Heart...the most vulnerable part of the entire body. Someone made my heart warm for the first time. Aiden's warmth drew me to him. But do I really deserve him? Do I deserve to be happy?

CHAPTER THREE

Chapter 3

"Aiden?" Aiden walked to Amelia and then turned towards his cousin. "Ashley, you are not needed here. Go and find a spot for yourself." "We will continue this conversation soon, dear senior." As Ashley walked away, giving Amelia another mean look. "You want me as your company?" "If you wish me to. It's not that I am going to force you to let me accompany you." Amelia was fidgeting with her hands, "We have known each other for just a day..." "And a night." Amelia smiled as she understood what trick Aiden was using. "I prefer to enjoy the party with my friends. They have known me for a considerable longer period of time than you." "Then make sure that you save a dance for me later." Amelia nodded. Her mobile rang again and she excused herself from the group. "Georgia, do you want me to accompany you tonight?" Georgia was taken aback by Noah's question and she nodded her head shyly as she felt her cheeks burning. "I will see you at 8 then." Noah walked away with Aiden who waved bye to the girls as he was a bit embarrassed.

"I would really love a partner for tonight" Jessica blunted. "I agree to disagree," Fiona said. "Everyone's opinion matters. Can't force anyone to feel the same way, can you?" Maria asked her sister. "If you really want a date for the party, you can try asking someone. After all, there is no such rule that a girl should ask a boy," Amelia reappeared. "I am embarrassed to ask anyone Amelia. I wouldn't have turned a guy such as Aiden down." "Yaniya, Maria just said, everyone's opinion matters. I think I stand up to." Jessica looked across the room her eyes stopped at a guy who was wearing boxing gloves and was playfully boxing his friend. "Amelia, I am going to try out your theory. Guys just wish me luck." Tanya beamed happily and showed her thumbs her as the others followed her. As Jessica went ahead and struck a conversation with the guy, Amelia turned towards the others, "Why don't you all give it a try?"

Before anyone could reply to Amelia about how much they wanted to try to talk and ask a boy out, they heard a loud surge of laughing from the opposite side of the room. Jessica held her head down and the guy she had just asked was laughing along with his friends. Amelia rushed as fast as she could with the others following her. When she reached Jessica, she saw fat drops of water, escaping her eyes. The guy seemed amused seeing Jessica cry and he shouted, "Fatso asked me to accompany her to the party." The others standing there were also laughing their lungs out. Jessica couldn't control anymore and she wailing loudly. Amelia hugged Jessica as she cried while the others were shamelessly laughing. Yaniya and the other girls looked angrily at the others and that seemed to quite most of them. Amelia handed the crying Jessica to Georgia and walked up to the guy and slapped him hard without hesitating. "What the hell girl? Did I offend you in any way?" "You insulted my friend here." "Insult? I just called her name, didn't I?" "Oh right! Then I apologize for hitting you, jerk." "Wait a minute. What did you call me?" "I called you by your name, just in case you forgot how that works." Amelia held Jessica's hand, "Let's go. People here are a mess." As they went away, the guy rubbed the surface of his cheek where Amelia had just hit him, "Now you got my attention, red head."

Jessica hadn't stopped crying. Tanya was patting her back while the twins were trying to console her. The people walking around were looking at these girls. Yaniya was standing at a distance with her hands folded. Amelia was again on her mobile. When she returned back she saw the others still consoling Jessica. She sighed angrily as she marched towards Jessica. "Are you planning to cry your eyes out? Was that guy really worth it? Do you think that anyone who was worth of you would actually make you cry? People in world have bigger and graver situations and they still smile and go through them. If you still think that your crying is going to make any difference to that guy, then you can continue crying," Amelia was yelling herself and stopped when she saw that everyone was looking at her, shocked.

Amelia took deep breaths and sat beside Jessica, holding her hands in a clasp. "I am sorry that I yelled my lungs out. Actually I was preoccupied with some of my personal things and I took it out on you. I don't want you feel that you were not enough and capable for that guy. He was just a rude guy, who doesn't know how to respect some people. Humans defend themselves attacking others. They use excuses like body, grades, ideal type etc. All of this nonsense just to amplify that you are not good enough for them. People like to believe that there would get someone better in their life. It was a stranger that said that to you but it hurts when your family says that to you. It might be your cousin saying that 'With that weight of yours, do you think that you would get any boyfriend?' Or your aunt, 'Think of losing some weight or no one will marry you.' Or your uncle, 'Studying is good but what about this fat?' People who make you feel low and make you feel you are less competent; don't deserve a place in neither your life nor your heart. You are beautiful the way you are and you really don't have to change anything in your life except discarding negative people."

Jessica hugged Amelia as she stopped crying. "I won't let anyone pull me down." "You promise that?" Jessica nodded and smiled. Yaniya pushed Georgia forward, "She bought you something." Jessica looked at Georgia who was holding a packet in her hands. "I noticed that you enjoyed eating cheeseburger so I bought you some." "Thanks, I love cheeseburger." Jessica happily took the packet and started munching on the burger as the others pampered her with words and patting on her head. Yaniya took Amelia to a side, "Why were you on the mobile the whole day?" "Umm...nothing. I was just looking for a part time job and luckily, I found one." "Where?" "Doccos."

Doccos was a café at a 15 minute walking place from the college. It was one of the biggest cafes in Hamlington. Getting a job there was considered difficult and if you were selected to work, then you might actually be possessing good luck. Thousands of applications used to flood in every time a vacancy notice was put on. Doccos was known be owned by a student studying in the same university as Amelia's. However, only the manager knew who it was as he was the most mysterious boss in the city. He was running a café at a young age and it was very successful. There was a well known rumor that the owner of the café had a dangerous temper. A rumor was generated when it was found out that some vases were accidently broken by some kids. After the manager had reported this to the owner via phone and it was instructed that the families of those kids would be banned from entering the café and the waiter serving that table was also fired.

"Are you sure, you can survive at Doccos?" "I am positive that I can make it. Why do you ask though?" "I had a friend who was working at Doccos. She had told me that even a lifetime in hell would be better than working at Doccos. Some costumers are extremely rude while some are perverted." "I guess some normal people also visit it. Don't they? And keeping these things aside, only Doccos is the place that pays more than the others in this area." Yaniya nodded her head, "You should still consider it once more." "I will but now, let's go and prepare our outfits."

"What theme should we follow?" Fiona asked the girls. "Was there any particular theme that was stated?" "No Yaniya, the notice clearly said that all the students living in a room together have to follow a similar theme" Amelia had just washed her face and joined the discussion. "How does bad girl sound?" Yaniya spoke up. "Schools had divided us into houses and now we are being divided in rooms." "I totally agree Georgia" Maria nodded while adding, "Old school?" "Mean Girls?" "Greek mythology?" Amelia was nodding her head as a no for these options. "Co...co...cot....cot....cot...cottage core." Everyone turned their heads in Tanya's direction as Amelia smiled and nodded her head in approval. "So let's get to work here."

Jessica pulled out a wig out from her bag. "Will I look good if I wear this?" "Yaniya, you will look beautiful in that. Trust me, I have 3 more wigs in my bag just in case I had a bad hair day." "Okay, I will wear it." Yaniya was selecting a wig to go with her dress. "We can still change the idea if you want." "No Georgia, I will be fine." Georgia was bubbling around the room. Never in her wildest dreams, had she ever thought a handsome guy like Noah, would ask her out on a dance. She remembered that she was shunned by her classmates for having a dark colour but what else can you expect from a typical ALL GIRL'S SCHOOL?

Amelia was going through everyone's clothes. She was searching for dresses in pale colours or dresses with little prints of flowers. So long, with Tanya's and Fiona's help, she had found three sets of each; pale and printed flowers. However, there was a problem for one dress. "See we have a cloth of pale and a cloth of printed and only if they are stitched together, one dress can be made." Amelia nodded to Fiona's observation. "Tanya you had given the idea, so decide which dresses will be worn by which one of us," Amelia gave the duty to Tanya who seemed embarrassed and happy to get this opportunity.

Laces, net cloth, scissors, threads and all the necessary material was taken out and the girls giggled as they smoothly went with each of the task given by Amelia. Tanya had decided that since Georgia had a date tonight, she had to look different from them and so the dress with half pale and half printed dress was to be made for her. Amelia had taken everyone's measurement and Maria and Yaniya were cutting the cloth as per the measurements she gave them. Jessica was making some rough designs for the dresses. Tanya and Georgia were sewing the dresses as Amelia had demonstrated to them and Fiona was pairing the shoes and getting some hair dressing materials from the shop near their campus.

"The dresses are ready" Amelia smiled as the others looked at them with big smiles on their faces. "I think that along with Amelia, we all can get a degree in Fashion Designing," Yaniya laughed at this remark by Maria. Amelia nodded her head and laughed with the others. Her phone ran and she rushed out with a pale expression. The others were too busy teasing each other to see that Amelia had turned white after coming inside. She was shaking and went to the bathroom. Jessica saw that Amelia had closed the bathroom door and she laughed, "Maybe Amelia wants to get ready soon that she doesn't miss a chance of impressing Aiden." The others laughed along with her as the tap in the bathroom was turned on and Amelia's cries went deaf on their ears.

On the other side of the campus, in the male dormitory, Aiden was continuously picking out suits and throwing them out. "Why in world I don't have anything good to put on?" "Aiden you are freaking me out. The first years have to dress according to their themes. Why are you so stresses out?" "Every guy is gonna were a suit like you. How will I look different than anyone then?" "I have a date night and you on the other hand, got REJECTED! But here we are, acting completely opposite of what is actually happening. Not everyone can be a prince." Aiden stopped in his tracks. "I know what I am going to wear."

AMELIA'S DIARY:

He said that he will come and live in Hamlington and I have to earn for him. Why? Cause I should be grateful that he has taken care of me. Care? Now I am going to play the role of the caretaker. Maybe after this day, I won't write anything about him in this diary because when I read this again, I want to remember the best time that I had here with my friends. Talking about friends, Aiden tried to ask me out on a dance date and I rejected him. Why did I do this? I am scared. I am sacred of this love and attention that has been directed towards me. I am not used to love. I am scared that this love will turn into hate someday. I can't handle negative emotions anymore.

The girls were excited for our first party. We dressed ourselves in cottage core and everyone was thinking if we could outdo the other dorms. I think this helped Jessica to forget her pain that she faced this morning. Public humiliation, one of the ways that can destroy a person completely. This world is too harsh and we are just teenagers. We should be taught to embrace everyone without thinking about their flaws. The way the society has set rules is totally wrong. I hate seeing someone getting laughed at their flaws. No human is perfect. Can we put an end to this judgmental thinking that has been passed from generations to generations?

CHAPTER FOUR

Chapter 4

The party was buzzing with the excited voices and the centre of the party had people slow dancing on the beats of romantic songs. Ashley's 'squad' was dressed as the Mean Girls, something that truly suited their personalities. They were wearing mini-skirts with crop tops and flashy jackets to match with and knee high cowboy boots to flaunt their long and toned legs. "I really like your style Ashley. Do you care for a dance with me?" "I am waiting for Kevin to ask me and by the way, who are you?" The guy, hung his head in disappointment and turned to leave. He had spent his entire time on Ashley and entertaining her and she said that she didn't remember his name. "Ashley, there is Kevin," Ashley's friend pointed at the hottest guy in the entire campus (obviously after Aiden and Noah).

Ashley tucked a string of her blond hair behind her ear and grabbed a drink as she walked near Kevin. She sat with her legs crossed and smiled looking at Kevin. Kevin's eyes wandered and settled at the girl before him. He smirked knowing that she wanted his attention and she had successfully gained it. He excused himself and went up to Ashley. "Can I the pleasure of buying you a drink?" Ashley bit her lip as she whispered 'BINGO' under her breath as she shyly nodded her head. Kevin had just turned behind when he noticed the same red head that had slapped him in the morning. The place was too crowded for him to see her face or the dress she was wearing but her hair were visible and he decided to make his way to the girl and make her pay for the slap.

Noah had taken the elegantly dressed Georgia to dance. He was standing with Aiden when he saw her enter. Her black hair tied firmly and tightly in a bun with flowers decorating the sidelines of her bun and her dress with the design of flowers and pale white was beautifully stitched diagonally as she had a light makeup on. Noah felt his heart skip a beat as she walked to him. He smiled at his friend who also looked mesmerized by Amelia. Every guy in the party had their eyes on Amelia since the moment she entered. A pale white off shoulder dress decorated with lace and net with her fiery red hair tied in princess braid. The fresh flowers were made into a semi tiara that made Amelia look like a forest princess. She smiled when she saw how Aiden had dressed. Aiden was wearing a white shirt and brown pants with matching shoes and had a cape of the same brown colour as the pants and shoes. He looked as the modern Prince Phillip from Cindrella. He bowed to Amelia as she smiled and bowed to him.

Yaniya who was wearing a pale royal blue dress with a wig on and had a flowery bracelet on her left hand was asked to dance by a painter as he said that he was mesmerized by her aura. Maria was asked by a fashion designer to dance with him and he complimented her on her choice of pretty flowers on her silvery white dress and hair wide open with flowers around as a crown. Jessica was standing aside enjoying the music in her flowery white dress with a slit and hair tied in bun and curls falling from the side decorating her face. Little did she know that a guy was staring at her and smiling from afar. Fiona was dancing in her pale avocado colour dress with the guy she was crushing on as the wind played with her prettily messy bun. Tanya was along with Jessica in her sky blue dress with tints of white flowers in her loose braided hair with small flowers lining downwards and she was taken aback when the captain of the soccer team asked her for a dance.

"Why a prince?" "For you my princess," Aiden chuckled as Amelia laughed along with him. "So may..." "You look really beautiful red head." Aiden was abruptly interrupted by Kevin. As soon as Aiden saw Kevin, his sweet smile turned into an angry scowl, "What are you doing here Kevin?" Kevin smirked as he ignored Aiden's question and walked to Amelia. "Kevin Gater and you are?" he bowed Amelia and took her hand and kissed it. Amelia pulled her hand back as swift as she could but Kevin grabbed her by her waist. He pulled her close and smirked, "Let's go dancing." Amelia bought her heel on Kevin's foot and as he cried in pain, Aiden pulled Amelia and held her by her waist, "Stay away from her and keep your dirty hands away from her." Amelia glared angrily at Kevin as she and Aiden walked away from the fuming Kevin.

The party was swaying on the tunes of 'My Heart Will Go On' as Aiden and Amelia had started dancing. Amelia was blushing and trying to avoid Aiden's handsome face. "You can look at me all that you want. No one is going to stop you and I don't have any objections." "Seems like you have a deal in mind Mr. Hourste?" "Well, maybe I want the same thing in return." Amelia smiled and bit her inner cheek, shyly. All of a sudden there was the sound of glass breaking and the music went off and people started gathering over a place, some meters away from Amelia and Aiden. Amelia couldn't understand the commotion. She saw a worried Georgia running to her followed by Noah. "Jessica...the guy..." Amelia understood what the breathless Georgia wanted to tell her and she ran and made her way to Jessica. Jessica was standing in the center of the circle and as expected, Kevin was laughing his lungs out.

A fellow student explained to Amelia that Kevin had walked up to Jessica and complimented her that the dress was looking beautiful on her and with that compliment, Jessica raised her hopes and smiled and blushed at Kevin. However, Kevin then started to insult her with sarcastic words and was now laughing at the 'dumb fatso' (as he named her). Amelia looked at Jessica with worry but when she saw Jessica's calm and quiet face, she breathed with relief. Kevin looked like a madman (which he was) as he was laughing all alone as the others looked at Jessica with pity in their eyes. "Do you really think, you dumb fatso that you...you will have a partner tonight? Loose that fat first. You look like a hippopotamus that is dressed for a circus show," Kevin said while laughing his lungs out. "Are you done?" Jessica asked in a cold and serious voice with her hands crossed which stopped Kevin and he looked at her with wonder in his eyes.

"Firstly look all around you jerk. No one is interested in this bullshit that you are talking about. Secondly, you need to learn one more thing, I DON'T NEED A PARTNER. Why? Why should I? Who made a rule that everyone needs a partner? I see no such anywhere," Jessica turned towards everyone, "Do y'all see anything like this written anywhere too?" The crowd shouted NO in union and that seemed to anger Kevin. "No one can deny that you are a fatso that is a burden on the ground that you stand on." "I don't deny that myself but atleast I weigh less that you and your whole WHY I SHOULD LOSE WEIGHT and HOW TO GET A

PARTNER crap. I need no one and I am happy as I am. That's the actual purpose of life. To be happy and you my dear jerk, haven't found happiness yet. Do you want this fatso to teach you how to be happy?"

The entire crowd cheered Jessica as Kevin stomped angrily outside and far away you could also see little fury Ashley following the love of her life. Jessica looked at Amelia with tears in her eyes and ran up to her. She hugged Amelia as Amelia patted her head and muttered 'Very well done' in her ears. Aiden looked at Amelia with both love and respect in his eyes. He smiled and asked Jessica to dance with him as Amelia mouthed a 'thank you' as they both disappeared in the crowd. Outside, the glorious Kevin sat defeated under a tree. He felt someone standing in front of him. "You are the girl from before. Do you want me to buy you a drink?" "Was it the red head that ruined your night?" "Do you know her?" Ashley nodded as she smirked at Kevin. She smiled thinking, 'Amelia, you made a little too many enemies now.'

"Excuse me" Amelia turned to face a stranger. He was good looking and he smiled warmly at her. "Yes?" "My name is Caden and I am a journalism student. Well, I was wondering if you could introduce me to that girl" he pointed towards Jessica. "Jessica?" "Yea, I would like to know more about her. Actually, I have been waiting to ask her for a dance the entire time and after the way she shut Kevin, I am even more interested in her." Amelia smiled 'Who says that fat girls like Jessica can't have a partner. Kevin should've seen how wrong he was.' She turned to the curious Caden, "Wait a minute." Amelia ran up to Aiden and Jessica, "Jessica, sorry but I really want to dance with Aiden." Jessica looked disappointed because Amelia spoke rude on purpose. "But..." Amelia smiled and spoke in her normal tone, "there is someone who wants to dance with you." Jessica's eyes went wide open as she couldn't believe at what Amelia said as she told the entire thing to Jessica.

"Jessica and Caden look so good, right?" "All of our friends look good except..." Aiden turned towards Amelia as she smiled and completed his sentence, "Us?" Aiden held Amelia's hand and they both started to dance leaving all the thoughts aside and unaware of the drama that would start from now on.

"Welcome to Doccos ma'am. May I take your order?" "I will have two cappuccinos and two chocolate pastries with sprinkles on please," the lady blunted. Amelia nodded and the lady went to a table as Amelia prepared her order. It was Amelia's first day at Doccos and being a fast learner, she quickly got used to the work. The shift started from 3PM (as the classes ended) and ended by 7PM. Amelia had received a text from Aiden in the morning, telling her that he will come to pick her at 6.45PM and then he wanted to take her to his favourite spot (basically a date). The girls had teased her about this in the morning but Amelia wasn't in it alone. Jessica and Georgia were also asked by Caden and Noah on a library date.

"I will have an Americano and Lady Amelia's time." Amelia turned to this strange request to see a grinning Aiden. She smiled sheepishly at him as she replied, "Sorry, I didn't hear you sir. Do you mind repeating it once more?" Aiden grinned and bent forward, "I want Americano and YOUR TIME." Amelia blushed and her mobile rang. She excused herself and went in the changing rooms. She came out within 5 minutes in her black skirt and white turtle neck blouse. Her hair tied in a messy bun and Aiden felt as he fell for her all over again. She smiled and started walking towards him but her legs were shaking strangely. Aiden had his eyes fixed on Amelia and he swiftly ran to Amelia as she fainted down. Amelia muttered 'Garden Hospital' as Aiden came to her. The last thing that Amelia remembered was Aiden carrying her in his arms as she blacked out completely.

Amelia's Diary:

I and Jessica had a little talk while the other girls were dressing themselves. I told her something that I had expected someone will tell me. I told her to fight her fears. To get rid of her insecurities and to embrace life and love herself just the way she was.

I thought some or the other adult would come in my life and tell me these things, like Amelia, you are good enough, you don't need to force things on yourself, you don't need to sacrifice your life for others, you need to live your own life in your way. The way you want to enjoy life. But it seems that before someone would say these words to me, I have already matured enough to understand them and act as my heart says. Maturity doesn't come with age, it comes with problems.

CHAPTER FIVE

Chapter 5

"Ms. Carol, she's here." Aiden looked confused. Amelia had uttered 'Garden Hospital' when she had fainted and he had bought her there. However, when he had just brought her in, the staff came rushing in and the nurses took her to 'Ms. Carol's' room. He had called Noah on his way so that Noah could tell the others. They were all on their way. Aiden felt tensed. The nurses had told him that Ms. Carol was Amelia's family doctor and she knew Amelia personally. Hence, the entire hospital was familiar with Amelia.

The door opened and Aiden rushed in. The first person he saw was Ms. Carol, who was a lady in her mid 40's. She smiled at him, "You must be Aiden. Amelia told me about you." "How is..." "Amelia is fine and I have given her a sleeping pill. It seems that she was too much stressed out." "How long will she be here?" "Five hours probably and there is something I need to ask you." "Where is Amelia?" All the girls had come with Noah and seemed anxious. "You all are?" "Ms. Carol they are Amelia's friends." "Amelia has friends? I mean, I am sorry but I haven't met any of Amelia's friends." "But doctor you knew me by my name." "Amelia told that Aiden had brought her here and that I should tell him to leave. She said that she will meet you tomorrow morning." Aiden turned towards the others,

"You all can go and sleep. Noah, take the taxi fare from me and check that they get safely to their dorms." "What about you?" Yaniya asked Aiden. "I will stay here."

"Good morning Amelia. You have made some really good friends." "What do you mean Ms. Carol?" "Aiden stayed her the entire night while the others are here with breakfast and clothes. They have asked for a leave for you from your part time and classes. Amelia, take some rest today and don't pick any call today." "Ms. Carol you know that if I don't pick his calls, he might come here and cause a scene." "However, promise me that you won't stress yourself too much. Your condition is improving rapidly and I don't want you to be skipping your meals and no stressing at all. I saw you as a malnourished child. Put on some more weight and you will be as good as new." "I will look like a pig then," Amelia grinned. "And since when did you become so self conscious? Since Aiden?" Amelia shook her head as a no and Ms. Carol ran her hand on Amelia's head as Amelia smiled cheerfully and ran to her friends. 'Poor child, why is her life the hardest of all?'

"You need to rest today!" "Jessica, I started working at Doccos yesterday and would it look good if I took a holiday on the second day of work?" "Okay go to your work but take atleast one of us with you so that we can keep an eye on you." "I am taking her and I will bring her back," Georgia proclaimed. Amelia sighed and muttered "Okay" as Georgia grabbed her hand and took her to the road leading Doccos. She texted Noah- 'I am with her.' Aiden had to know that Amelia was safe and Noah, Georgia's boyfriend. They had clicked soon as they had met and Noah knew that he would be wasting his time if he didn't ask Georgia out. Georgia answered positive and they were the first couple in this group.

Doccos was packed with people more than the day before. Georgia was sitting on a table that was close to Amelia's counter. People came and the orders were poured. Amelia saw a group of 7 girls enter together, their hands locked into each other. "Your order ladies?" " Three large mushroom pizzas and seven large vanilla coffees." They turned around and halted. "Trash bag, what are you doing here?" Georgia flinched when she saw the girls. A cold shiver ran down her spine as she gulped the water down her throat.

PAST MEMORIES:-

"This is your new classmate Georgia. Welcome your new friend with a round of applause" the teacher introduced a 15 year Georgia who had migrated from her hometown to Hamlington. She was a popular girl back in her hometown and was all excited to make new friends here in the fresh air of Hamlington. The teacher was kind and the students were all from rich families. The girls smiled at her and whispered something in each other's ears. Georgia was thinking that she will make a lot of friends in this girl's school. It was just 5 miles away from her house and she could cycle her way to the school.

Georgia sat on the seat next to a girl wearing a pretty pink skirt and lavender blouse. She smiled at her to which the girl raised an eyebrow at her and rolled her eyes. 'Maybe she is shy to talk to me,' Georgia thought to herself. She attended the classes and during the recess went to the girl and held her hand forward, "Hello, I am Georgia. I want to be your friend." The girl glared at Georgia with anger and then called her two friends, "This trash bag," turning to Georgia she continued, "A trash needs to be in the dustbin and you don't know your rightful place. Do you want me to show you how to sit in your right place?"

Georgia had heard about school bullies but this was her first encounter with some. She felt insecure and she turned to leave when the girl caught her by her collar and pulled her back. “You said that you wanted to be friends with us, didn’t you?” the girl took a water bottle and emptied it on Georgia. Georgia was drenched in water from head to toe. “First rule of friendship, make your friends laugh” the girls laughed loudly as the other students ignored this scene. After that, for the rest years of her life, until she came to the university, these three girls bullied her on several occasions. Sometimes they would throw water on her or sometimes they would draw on her with markers. On other occasions, they would cut her hair and on other they would make her eat rotten leftovers. The other students never interfered in these matters and soon the ‘popular’ and ‘cheerful’ Georgia disappeared and in her place, ‘scared’ and ‘insecure’ Georgia took her place. That’s why when Georgia had joined the new university, she was scared how the others would treat her but to her joy, Amelia and the others treated her very well and she was regaining her old self.

PRESENT MOMENT:

Until now, the same old three girls were standing in front of her. The same ones due to whom she had to take consultation classes and medications. She had spent the two months of her holidays just to become ‘normal’ and muster courage to start her life anew at the university and now these months of practice seemed fruitless. Amelia was confused at this sight. With the order ready for the customers, she walked up to them, “Your order, kindly pay your bill.” “This trash will pay the bill. We have missed her. Won’t you pay for us?” the leader asked her. Amelia raised her eyebrow, “She will not pay anything. You are the ones that gave the order, so pay yourselves." "Waitress, stay away from this. The girl is our friend, so will do anything for us." "Georgia, do you owe anything to them?" Georgia was shivering with fear but she managed to nod her head, saying a no. "Come near me," Amelia took her friend behind her and glared at these three girls, "If she were your friend, she would've been happy. You called her a trash bag and she is shivering at your sight. Do you really think I can fall such a lame excuse?"

"Maybe, you are confident due to this redhead trash bag. Waitress, stay away or we have show how we treat outcasts and you are too pretty to be friends with someone as ugly as her." "You are not bad looking yourself but I have never met someone with such ugly and sick mindset as yours. You call her trash bag? You stink. Your mentality stinks. Your order is cancelled. Get out from her." "You dare to tell my cousin to get out of from my own café? Where do you get this confidence from red head?" Amelia couldn't believe that the jerk, Kevin Gater was the owner of this café. And on top of that this stubborn and arrogant girl was his cousin. 'The world is indeed a small place.' Kevin was not alone. He was arms-in-arms with Ashley who was smirking at her. Amelia took a deep breath and decided to behave professionally as the crowd was taking an interest in the commotion. "Welcome Sir and Ma'am. May I take your orders?" "Played like a true pro player Amelia. After all, you are a cunning vixen. Ashley, my love, what do you want to have?" "Cappuccino and pastries." "You heard her and about the commotion that was going on earlier, my cousin was not wrong. This girl is trash for sure." Amelia glared at this entire group and held her friend's hand and took her to the counter as she prepared the order. The five people sat on the nearest table and laughed as they ridiculed this duo of a redhead and trash bag.

Georgia was still shaking when Amelia had served her 'boss and his minions'. "How long have you kept all of this in?" "Four years." "Tell me what you should have done if you were alone in this situation?" "I would've called you or Noah. You both would save me from them again." "And do you think that we are super heroes? You need other people to stand up for you? Why don't you take a stand for yourself? We can back you, support you, but fighting for your own needs, your own dignity and finding your own voice is essential. You are preoccupied by the opinions of these girls." "But I am scared. They laugh at me, they have hit me, bullied me to amuse themselves. They laugh seeing others in pain and living in fear." "You got your own solution." "What are you talking about?" "Fear. If you don't fear them, they can't have any control over you. Once, you break free from this shackles of fear, you can achieve happiness and freedom. Don't let anyone make you feel inferior or disheartened. If anything happens again, stand up for yourself and remember that you have me, your friends and a caring boyfriend to back you. You should smile and work hard for your future. You are capable and don't need anyone in your life just to show you that you have to be dependent on them. I trust you and I know that you will be brave and solve your own problems." Georgia smiled at her and hugged Amelia. "If you keep hugging her like that, I will surely feel jealous" Georgia broke from the embrace to see her boyfriend grinning with his best friend who was (as always) staring at Amelia. "Trash bag, come here."

Amelia's Diary:

I find it unbelievable sometimes that there are a certain group of human beings that like to prey on other human beings fear and make them a laughing stock in front of their peers. They just don't make fun of a person but they install fear in them. Fear that leads to a sense of insecurity and that insecurity threatens the person's self confidence. The person starts to hate herself and then falls in a deep denial and can't escape it without a ray of hope. What is a ray of hope for such a person? It's someone who accepts the person as she is and lending her a hand or an ear. Parents should be that ray of hope but nowadays, which parent has time for her kid that is facing depression or bullying? Some kids even hide that fact that such things are happening to them. And then there are some so called 'Friends' who side with the ones with power and the pit goes on deeper and the person falls in a much more denial.

Finally there are only two outcomes of this situation. Either, the person sinks so deep in depression that she never surfaces to wait for the ray and even if she gets one, she refuses to embrace it or the person learns to stand for themselves and that person, becomes their own ray of hope. I hope that every single person learns to stand for their own self cause there is no one who will do it for you.

CHAPTER SIX

Chapter 6

"Who is that rude brat calling? Amelia you?" Amelia shook her head in negative as Noah saw that Georgia was walking towards the 'rude brat' that he had just mentioned. As he was going behind her, Aiden held his arm and signaled him not to interfere in this conversation. Noah was glaring at the group as Georgia went up to them. Aiden looked at Amelia who looked calm and at the same time curious. One thing that Aiden had learnt about Amelia that she knew how to make a person face her fears with ease and that was something that the society doesn't teach you, experience does. "Trash bag, pass those tissue papers to us." Georgia turned to look at Amelia who gave her an encouraging smile. "Get them yourself," Georgia blunted out. Ashley raised her eyebrow as she whispered something in Kevin's ear. He glared at Amelia as she smirked at him. "Trash bag, how dare you talk back at me? Did you forget the rules that you should follow if you wanted to be my friend? OBEY ME!!!" Georgia smiled, "Why should I? Who are you?" The girl looked offended and stood up. She walked to Georgia and raised her hand to slap her but before she could slap Georgia, a hand was brushed hard on her face. Georgia had stuck a slap on her face "I have had enough of your so called orders and now I don't feel the obligation to keep obeying those orders. Your father is a rich man. Ask him to get you your personal servant and if you dare raise another finger at me in the future, I will make sure that you regret it." "How dare you, a lowly trash bag, slap me? Do you wish to die that badly?" the girl again raised her hand but Amelia held it. She had walked behind Georgia when she slapped the girl. "Keep your filthy mindset in your pocket. Don't you dare ever approach my friend and if I get to know that you are lingering around her as a parasite, I will call the police and sue you for bullying." Kevin stood up at this but before he could say anything Amelia handed her badge to him, "I quit."

"I am sorry Amelia that you had to quit because of me" Georgia, Noah, Aiden and Amelia were sitting in a cafe opposite from Doccos. It was a small cafe named 'Olivia'. "Georgia, I am genuinely happy for you and you are not the reason I quit. It was Kevin's café and it would have been extremely foolish of me to work their just for money. Who knows that he might have ordered me around with all kinds of errands and I might have become a doll that danced as he wanted. I wouldn't give anyone any reason to control me...ever again!" Aiden looked at Amelia with great curiosity in his eyes as she had emphasized, 'Again?' "Well, this café isn't bad, is it?" Noah commented. Amelia looked around. It was not grand as Doccos but looked peaceful. It was half the size of Doccos excluding the part outside. That meant if this portion was used, it would be enough to accommodate large crowds. The owner was an old lady and the cafe had a sign saying, 'Anyone interested in buying, kindly contact the owner.' "I want to buy this place," Amelia said as the others widened their eyes at her.

"The price is not much because this place is not much worth. I have been working her since the age of thirty one and today I am a sixty five year old lady. I have invested both, my time and energy. This place is a part of me. Selling it makes my heart pain. However, things must move on. You can convert this space as per your liking. About the payment, pay half the price now and I will hand all the documents to you but you have to make sure that you give half the amount later." Amelia nodded her head in affirmation as she took out a cheque book. She looked at the lady, "How much do I need to pay now?" "$40,000 and the same amount later after the entire documents are transferred to you. The legal procedures will take about a week and then you can start working in your own place." Amelia smiled and nodded her head cheerfully as she scribbled the amount on the cheque and handed it over to the lady as she stood and followed the lady as she called her lawyer. Aiden was amused at this scene. He looked at Georgia and Noah who were holding each other's hands and Noah was comforting his love just by his eyes as she was gazing lovingly at him, "You both get going. I and Amelia will try to complete most of the legal procedures and come by 7PM." Noah looked at Georgia to answer as it was her decision to make. "Aiden and Noah, you both get going, I will not leave Amelia. I will call you when we reach the dorms." Aiden sighed as he walked out with Noah, looking disappointed. But he turned to see a beaming Amelia talking with the lady.

The procedures were fully completed within 4 hours as the lawyers of both the parties were cooperative and had a good coordination. Amelia had called Ms. Carol as her another witness, with Georgia being one and had all the documents under her name and she had to wait for atleast three days to start the shop. She had taken Ms. Carol's advice on this matter and Georgia had seen that these two had an unbreakable bond and adored each other. One might mistake that these two where mother and daughter. Ms. Carol had suggested that for these three days, she should renovate the entire place as per her liking. Surely, that wasn't a work of three days but could be completed within seven days. Within that time, Amelia should promote her café, find investors, workers and the stock for just a month. The first month was to be treated as a trial period and that would determine whether the café could last in the tough competition by Doccos.

Amelia had thanked everyone for their patience and support and she and Georgia walked out of the café, arm in arm. "Amelia, I might sound too rude and curious and I know that it is not right to prey into someone else's life, but you said that you needed money really badly but today you spent around $50,000 in an instant and that surprised me." Amelia smiled sadly, "When my mom died, she had left $200,000 of her insurance money under my name as the nominee. I was 4 years old that time and I was told about this amount by the bank notice when I became of a legal age. But by then, I had learnt to earn on my own to survive, so I have saved that money for some important purpose. However, I felt that I shouldn't wait more to use the money. It would be wasted if I didn't use it afterall everything has an end and then again, I didn't waste my money, if I don't do well, Doccos will probably buy the place to expand its area. So it's a win-win situation." "What was the important purpose you had saved the money?" "Marriage," Amelia giggled and Georgia smiled at her witty remark but her heart knew that Amelia was lying about this. "We are at the dorms, call your boyfriend and inform him or else he would have a sleepless night." "I will tell the one who courts you too," Georgia teased Amelia, as Amelia blushed thinking about Aiden and ran up the steps as Georgia took a walk while talking to Noah on the call.

In the morning, the girls were all ready and sitting in the cafeteria, enjoying their delicious breakfast while Amelia was continuously browsing the net. She was the only one on the table that had an untouched plate. Jessica had finished eating and saw the 'CONCENTRATED' Amelia. She picked up Amelia's plate, "Amelia, open your mouth" she instructed. Amelia was so engrossed with her laptop that she just listened to Jessica without even looking at her. Jessica stuffed the sandwich in Amelia's open mouth. Amelia reacted to this quick and quickly placed her hand on the sandwich, which was partially hanging from her mouth and could fall on the ground anytime due to the gravitational pull. "First eat your breakfast and take the meds. The laptop isn't running away and we don't want you to fall ill again" Jessica scolded Amelia. Amelia hung her head down in shame and started eating the food. After she had finished, she looked at a smiling Jessica who gave her a thumbs up and patted her back. Amelia looked at the time. It was still an hour for their classes to start and she had a big load of work to do. She looked at the girls who were joking and laughing around her. She loved this atmosphere. The cheerful environment was taking all the pain away from her slowly. She stood up with the laptop in her hand, "Come with me."

"Ol....oli.....oli....oliv.....Olivia? This....p....p...p....place is s...s....s...so bea...beau...beau....beauti....beautiful!!!" Tanya exclaimed. Fiona and Maria along with Yaniya were already going over the entire place while Jessica and Georgia were talking about the happenings that had led Amelia to buy this place. "So this entire place costs $80,000?" Yaniya asked when Georgia had told everything to them. Amelia nodded her head shyly. "Don't you think that with a competitor as strong as Doccos, your business will be in loss?" "Maria, I surfed the net and found out some amazing details about this place. It was originally a bakery and was auctioned for $50,000 to the lady. This place was profitable until Doccos came here. They had asked the lady to sell this place to them for a much higher rate than she sold it to me. But the lady has sentimental attachment to this place and didn't want her competitor to take over here. If the trial period of my business, which is one month, doesn't go well, I will sell this place, either to an interested party or Doccos. The final papers will be handed to me day after tomorrow but before all that, I want to ask you guys for something." "What do you mean?" Fiona asked.

"That is all for today class. I will be posting an assignment about the various fabrics and you have to submit a detailed report about them along with the samples. For the next class, remember to bring your sketchpads and any fabric of your choice. The length of the fabric has to be around 2 meters. The other basic essential tools like needles, threads, tailor's chalk and pins have to be necessarily in your bag all the time. The class is dismissed. Have a happy weekend." Amelia grabbed her bag and ran as soon as the professor left the class. Ashley wrinkled her nose, "Urchin" as Amelia passed her. Amelia, even though hearing an insulting word, ignored her and ran down the stairs. She saw Maria and Yaniya were already outside the main entrance when Amelia reached them. "Wh...where are the others?" Amelia asked, her lungs crying out for oxygen. "Fiona and Jessica are gone to buy paints while

Tanya and Georgia have gone to the carpenter. We have to go to buy curtains, table cloths, utensils and the other necessities." Amelia smiled at the details that Maria gave her. She had asked the girls to help her to design the café with her and they had agreed to it. Georgia had asked whether they could involve Noah and Aiden in this plan to which Amelia had said a strict no. She didn't feel like involving the two everytime. She didn't want to be dependent on anyone else and had rejected this idea straightaway.

At quarter to 5 the girls were together at Olivia. Jessica, Maria and Georgia had decided the colors in which the entire place was supposed to be painted in. A warm peach color was to be painted to the walls, both the inner walls and the outer walls; however the roof would be painted in white. The café had an open kitchen area opposite to the entrance and a display counter in front it. The area was 1,450 sq feet including the kitchen and the counter. The girls had discussed their working strategy. They were going to work in teams of two, making three groups. Being an odd figure, one team would have three members. Amelia and Fiona were going to paint the kitchen, Yaniya, Jessica and Maria had to paint the main café area and Georgia and Tanya were painting the outer walls. The girls had covered the wooden flooring (which was surprisingly in an excellent condition) with plastic that Yaniya had bought. Wearing their aprons, gloves, caps and masks on, they started painting the entire place.

"Are we welcome here?" Noah walked inside the painted Olivia with some snacks in his arms, to find the girls sitting at the center of the place, all exhausted. Aiden came in with cold drinks in a transparent bag. Amelia was resting her head on Maria's shoulder. To be precise, she was already asleep. Georgia signaled Noah and Aiden to be silent and took the refreshments from them. The girls opened the snacks very slowly without making any noise; least it woke Amelia. Noah and Aiden went all around the place. The girls had done the job wonderfully within a span of 5 hours. The dorm rooms were supposed to close at 10.30 PM. "You guys have done a really excellent job. However, we have to hurry or else all of us will be locked out and our parents will be called" Noah made his point clear. "But, Amelia just slept half an hour ago, what do we do about her? Shall we wake her?" "No Jessica, I will carry her to the dorm" Aiden blunted as all girls smiled at this romantic gesture.

"Young man, you can't enter the ladies dorm. You have to wake her," the warden was stubborn. "She is tired after continuously working for 5 hours. You can come with me. I will just lay her on her bed and come out quickly. Please let me do it fast or my warden won't let me in" Aiden pleaded the warden as she sighed and signaled him in. Aiden followed Yaniya as she quickly opened the dorm room and showed him Amelia's bed. He took a piece of paper nearby. Wrote something on it and placed it under Amelia's pillow and wished everyone goodnight as he ran to his dorm.

Amelia's Diary:

I woke up in the middle of the night to find myself carefully tucked in my bed. I couldn't recall how I got here as I fell asleep in the café. I looked around to see that all the others were already in their dreamland. They all had helped me a lot since the past few days and today was a big help, the biggest I could ever imagine. I need to thank them properly for their help as I am indebted to them. It is easy to make friends but it is hard to find those friends that stand by you in your hardships and trials. I am grateful to my fate that I met such wonderful six girls who are always by my side and never fail to help me. Ms.

Carol was right, I made really good friends.

I felt thirsty, so I walked to the table where we have placed the water cooler and drank some water. As I came to the bed and adjusted my pillow, I saw a note. It said,

"You look beautiful even when you are asleep.

Goodnight, firefly.

Aiden."

I smiled at the note. These small romantic moments make me think that I am the main character of a novel who was being courted by her first love. It's amusing to think, but Aiden IS my first love. I have worked out my feelings and I am sure how I feel about him. Firefly, he thought of a unique nickname. It suits me very well as, I'd like to think that I take light with me wherever I go, I make people smile.

CHAPTER SEVEN

Chapter 7

"First, we'll complete our pending assignments and then go to the café," Amelia strictly told the whimpering girls. From the morning, the girls were asking to go to the café. If they started from early the morning, they would complete more than half of the work. Amelia had rejected this idea completely. She didn't want the girls to ignore their studies and just focus on the café. The café was her responsibility and she didn't want to burden the others with her workload. The help of painting the café was more than enough but now seeing their excitement and genuine feeling of helping her out, made her heart melt. The others, seeing that she was serious about completing their class work and then the café, sat on their chairs and started writing as fast as they could.

Amelia opened her laptop and then her mailbox. She had ordered some decorative items for the café and they were supposed to be delivered at Olivia around 2PM. They would reach there by that time. It was only 8 in the morning. Opening her Microsoft Word, Amelia started typing about the various fabrics, their origin, their ancient history, the place of importance where the fabrics were used most and after she finished her assignment, she picked her bag, "I am going to take the printing from the machine

on the first floor and I will go to the cloth market from there. I will go the café directly after purchasing my material needed for the assignment. Tanya has the other key of the café. After and only after you all have completed the assignments, you will go to the café. There might be a delivery. Take care of it if I don't reach there on time."
"O...o...ok Am....Ame...Amel.....Amelia. Be s....safe. W..we w..will do ever....everyth....everything pr...propl....properly" Tanya showed her a thumbs up.

After printing her assignment, Amelia hired a taxi and went to the cloth market. She got an unpleasant call on her way. She transferred $100 to the number even without picking up the call and got off at her destination. The cloth market was ridiculously empty. It was 11.30AM and the market still seemed pretty bare. She went to the nearest shop. A girl greeted her with a smile on her face. The owner was a man, who was sitting in a corner and eyeing Amelia strangely. The girl asked Amelia what she was searching for and Amelia gave her details for the specific cloth, its color and the length. The owner got up from his seat and walked to them and greeted Amelia. "Let me help you. Sasha is a new part timer here and she might not be able to help you." Amelia nodded her head, making it seem that she understood the situation; however, she saw that the atmosphere here had gotten pretty awkward. She turned her head to the other side, walked to the other side and inspected the other cloth materials. She thought she heard a whimper, so Amelia looked at the part timer. The owner was unaware that Amelia was looking at them and to her great horror, Amelia saw the owner touching the girl. She didn't waste any moment and she ran to the owner. The owner suddenly panicked, "Wait a moment young lady. Let me search the material." Amelia held the girl's hand and pulled her behind her. She looked at the owner with disgust in her eyes and slapped him hard. The owner widened his eyes in anger and was about to slap Amelia but stopped in his tracks seeing that Amelia had pulled her mobile out and was recording him. "What do you think you are doing here? How dare you slap a man that is your father's age? Have you got no shame?" The man shouted loudly at her. This commotion caused the other shopkeepers to look intently at them. "I have no shame in slapping a man who is a sexual abuser. Have you got no shame in touching a girl that might be your daughter's age? And on top of that, you dare to teach me shame?" Amelia turned at the girl, "You too are responsible. You should have slapped him the first time he dared to touch you. This is sexual abuse and you are the victim and yet you continue to be one?" "I didn't have any choice. I am the sole bread winner in the family of three. I have got younger siblings to feed to. It has only been two month since I have started working here and I haven't even received any payment." Amelia glared at the owner, "Pay her the due amount. She won't be working for you anymore. She will work with me in my café."

"This is Sasha and I met her at the cloth market. She is going to work with us." Amelia had bought Sasha to Olivia. At first she was pissed at Amelia for making her lose her job. 'Dignity?' 'Honour?' 'Respect?' Which job offered it along with a good payment? She was paid $200 a month at the shop and then she was in a taxi with a stranger with $500 in her pocket. $100 was a compensation fee for the mental and physical harassment. Actually, Amelia had threatened the man to pay her extra money or else she would viral the video on social media. Amelia then took Sasha to another shop and bought the dress. She hired a taxi and made Sasha sit along with her. Then she made a deal.

Sasha would be a full time employee and her monthly salary would consist $350. Sasha agreed to it happily when Amelia said that she and her younger siblings could dine for free in the café until Sasha feels to do so.

Amelia got a call and she went out while the others came up to Sasha and chatted with her. They got to know the entire episode within a few minutes. "We should've been there. I would've kicked the man right on his face" said Yaniya angrily. "Well, it doesn't matter now. I am glad that Amelia came there today and dragged me out from that hell. She is kind, helpful and a good person by her heart. I am glad that I am here." "Was someone talking about my heart? Well it has a big hole that's why I need to fill it with compliments" Amelia giggled as she came in. "No one is talking about you. You just ask to be spoilt by us. If you want to be spoilt so bad, go to Aiden. That boy will spoil you endlessly," Yaniya teased her as Amelia laughed and hugged her. "There is a delivery for Ms. Araste. Is she in here?" "Well it seems our delivery is here, let's get to work shall we girls?" Amelia walked out with the others behind her.

15 plants, wooden furniture (consisting 40 chairs, 25 tables, big display cupboard), clock, table cloths, 20 fairy lights, many books and about 200 pink chart papers. "Sasha and Tanya, you both decide the positions of the plants. Make it look simple and aesthetic. Don't make it look too crowded. Fiona and Georgia arrange the chairs and tables along with the table cloths. Maria and Jessica, sit in one corner and I want you to cut these chart papers in heart shapes. Yaniya, you and me are gonna decorate the entire place." "And do you need us?" Aiden walked in as the girls eyed Amelia, who controlled her blushing handed him a cutter. "There is a huge box outside. It has a fake tree in it

and it branches. Assuming that you are here, I think Noah is outside parking the car. I want you to take out the fake tree and assemble it together. Call me out once that is done and I will tell you what to do later." "Okay madame," Aiden bowed to Amelia and kissed her hand as he went out.

It took them the entire afternoon and the evening to complete all the arrangements. Every single one of them had done their job excellently. Plants were placed at regular intervals. Tables and chairs carefully arranged with their table cloths. The fairy lights made the café look magical and the display cupboard was filled with books. Aiden and Noah had gone shopping for refreshments with Georgia after fixing the fake tree (along with its branches) in the ground after digging it and placing some iron rods for support. Then they had inserted the tree's bottom part inside the ground and sealed it with cement. The fake tree was now as strong as a real one, with it 'roots' deep inside the ground. The hearts were also ready. Amelia and Jessica had gone to the dorm to bring the entire stock of utensils while Yaniya and Sasha had gone shopping for a week's business. The rest of the girls were wiping the glasses of the windows and the display counter when the door opened.

"This is it? It looks so weird and childish. Gosh! You girls really don't have any taste" Ashley was inside Olivia with her boyfriend, Kevin. "I agree. Someone said that this place might become a competition for Doccos but after seeing this, I am sure that Doccos will be safe forever." "N...no...no...........o...o...on...one ask.....k...k...asked for.....y....y...yo...you...your...." "Just shut up you slow poke. I got too tired to hear even a single sentence from you. You should try becoming a baby sitter. The child will get bored of you within no time and would sleep real easily. Or else you should stop talking at all. For people like you, sign language is the best option. You have got three benefits. First, you don't have to talk. Second, no one will laugh at you and third, everyone will pity you cause they will think you are mute." "And who the hell wants your pity?" Amelia burst into the café. Jessica was standing behind her, glaring dead in Kevin's eyes. "Kevin, no one invited you here and you are not needed here. I don't see that anyone ordered a glass of your opinion. Get out respectfully and don't come back," Amelia furiously shouted at Kevin. "I wasn't too eager to come here. Someone messaged me that the old lady had sold this place to a girl and she might be a tough competitor for me. I came to check it but it's untrue. You? You worked for me. It's hard to think that a lowly peasant from the countryside, challenging someone like me? Did you and your friends ask for donations to afford this place? This is so sad. I would've lent you some of my pocket money. You needn't go begging to this instant." "I w...w....w...wasn't mmin...min....minding until you www...w..we...were talking ill to me bbe...bbb...bec...bec...because I genuine...e...e...ely don't give a sh...sh...shit about yo..you...you..your opinions abo....ab...about me but you sh....sh...sh...shouldn't dare to talk to Amelia like t....h...this. You ha....ve.....ve...have a heart that only kkk...kk...knows to p...p...pum...pu...pump bloo...ood...blood and ke...e...ee....keep you aliv...v....alive while Amelia's he...hea...hear...heart knows to mmm....mm...ma...make other people's heart....w.....w....w.....warm and ssh...sh...sh...sh...she knows how to mmak..mak...make someone sm..sm...sm...smil...smile. People like you...w...w...wh...wh...who demotivate other...s...s.s without any sha...sha...sham....shame are boring. You jud...ju...ju....judge people cause y..yo...yo...you got no bett....t....t.....ttt....t...better things to do...an....ann...annn...ann...an...a...and as for a competition t..t...to Doccos, mind m...m...m...my words, O...li...li....Olivia will do better th...th..tha...th...than any other café in the en...en...ent....enti....entire Hamlington." "Fine!!! Whatever you say stutterer. Let's get going Ashley."

Ashley turned and walked arms in arms with her boyfriend, who seemed flustered because of the insult. Ashley was angry at Kevin due to his inability of giving a powerful comeback to these losers. While walking past Amelia, Ashley brought her heel on Amelia's foot. Amelia let out a cry and the others ran to her. Yaniya shouted Ashley's name aloud but Jessica stopped her saying, "Dogs know how to bite." Ashley was going to say something but she saw her cousin coming from the opposite side and she picked up her pace. Kevin drove them out as Amelia took off her shoes. The heel hadn't struck too deep as to break any tissue or skin layer but there seemed a big blue bruise at the place of the injury. Aiden took an ice bag from the refrigerator as the others were filling him with the incident. He didn't say a word and handed Tanya the ice bag to apply it to Amelia's foot. Then he dialed a number, "Good evening uncle. I am sorry to call you this late in the night but Ashley has being troubling a classmate of hers unnecessarily. She has caused her a lot of accidents recently and I hope that after this call, you will tell her the right from wrong because if she abuses her power as the daughter of the treasurer of the university, I won't think twice before informing the police about it. I am sorry if I sounded rude but this is the only message I like to convey." Aiden hung up even before hearing his uncle's reply. The others were glaring at him with pure anger except Amelia. She had the look of betrayal in her eyes. "Ashley is my cousin. Her dad is the treasurer of our university. I wasn't able to tell you about this because I wanted to protect her from the prejudices of other people but whatever she has been doing to you, Amelia, has made me frustrated. I am sorry." Amelia stood up and smiled sadly at him. "Is there anything about you that I still don't know? Something else that you are hiding from me? From all of us?" Aiden held his head down in shame. The only thing that Aiden was still hiding from them was that he was the son of the owner of the university (this wasn't related to any incident and so he hadn't felt the need to boost his power in front of anyone).

Amelia picked her shoes and handed the keys to Jessica, "I am tired and I will be returning to the dorm now. When everyone comes, tell them to eat the snacks that Georgia had bought. I will treat you guys after the business starts. Tanya, take care of the café for me please." Aiden walked towards Amelia with his hand stretched forward, "Aiden...don't. I need some time to think alone. I will text you once I sort things out." Amelia closed the door and ran barefoot to her dorm room. She closed the door and making sure that she was alone in the room, she started crying loudly. She cried and cried until there were no tears left in her eyes. She got up, went to the bathroom and showered. Wearing her pajamas, she lay on the bed for some time. After around twenty minutes, she sat up in her bed, opened the drawer near her and pulled out an ointment. Slowly she applied it, very gently and carefully. It wasn't the first time that she had got hurt. She had been hurt a lot more times before and that too very badly. She took a look at the small pouch in the drawer, pulled it out and ate her medicines. It had been so many years, that she didn't even remember when she first ate these medicines. In the past 3 years, along with her regular medicines, she had started taking sleeping, depression and anxiety pills too. These made her feel better as she could function properly due to them. Her mobile lightened with a notification. On opening the message she read it as,

I am sending some sandwiches along with Georgia. We would be glad if you ate something before you sleep. Aiden is sorry for what he did. We would be glad if you came to cheer us for tomorrow's basketball match.

Goodnight and take care :)

Amelia switched her mobile off and took the blanket on her head as the sleeping pill started its effect.

Amelia's Diary:

I won't talk about sexual abuse as only from the point of view of a female. Men suffer this problem too. You know why is it considered it as a problem even when it isn't one? We don't talk about it to anyone. The fear of what the society thinks of us, keeps us shut, keeps our thoughts shut.

Sasha was trying to fill her family's basic needs and for this she needed to earn a livelihood. Then why do some people think that needy people like her are easy targets for their wrongful and sinful deeds? She chose to work honestly and then was taken advantage of. I slapped the man cause the scene disgusted me. However, it would really make me happy if it were Sasha who slapped the man in my place. I would have been happy if girls or boys; who are abused, take a stand for themselves. I loved it today when Tanya spoke for herself. She showed us that she is not a coward. I am grateful that she thinks highly of me.

I learnt this today that we can't let anyone take a stand for us because there is no one in the world who is capable like one self. Aiden hid the fact that Ashley was his cousin to protect her from our biased opinions. Really? He wanted to protect himself from the fact that his cousin was the one

troubling the whole time and that he wouldn't be welcomed by us. To be honest, this thing has surprised me. I try to get along with people even when I know that my flaws might distance them from me. Aiden lied when he said that he was protecting Ashley. He didn't want us to distance away from him. I think I should make it clear to him that we won't leave him just because Ashley is his cousin, cause we truly appreciate his company.

CHAPTER EIGHT

Chapter 8

It had been two months since Olivia had started and sure as Tanya had predicated, it was a huge success. Doccos remained as its competitor but it grew weaker everyday. The workers from Doccos, who were continuously reminded that they were nothing but mere workers, grew sick of the attitude and joined Olivia. The main concept that attracted people was the fake tree. Before Olivia had begun, Amelia had installed that tree with Aiden's and Noah's help. The tree was decorated with fairy lights but this wasn't all. Amelia had hung long strings from the branches to the ground. The pink chart papers, which were cut into heart shapes, were kept at the entrance. The concept was that when a person goes out, he/she will pick out a heart, write any message for any person and sign their own name and the person who it is addressed to.

There were about hundreds of hearts with messages every single day. The customers used to come in, order, pick out any book that they liked and sat reading it till the order arrived. There were certain bookworms, mostly ordered a cup of coffee and sat reading for hours together. Doccos had been providing free wifi since it was inaugurated. Amelia wanted people to detach from the electronic gadgets for some time in her café. Today was the day when Amelia was going to introduced something new in the café. She had been planning to do it since a long time and now she could do it. Aiden and Yaniya had gone along with Sasha's siblings to bring the 'gift'. She had gone to the basketball game and had understood Aiden's fear of being ignored by her. She was again good friends with him while the others teased her that soon this friendship will take a romantic turn to which Amelia always said, "It won't work between us."

Ashley had kept their distance away from her since Ashley's father had reprimanded her and taken away all her cards. Now the Ashley, who had once made fun of thrift shops, seemed a usual customer at the local thrift shop. However, her ego was still the same. Kevin seemed bored of her and broke up with her soon enough. He was not seen since a period of more than a month. Some said that he had travelled to his family to take care of some real estate deals. Life was pretty smooth around the campus now and things seemed great. Amelia got two messages on her mobile to one, she sent her regular $100 and to the other, it seemed to fill her with happiness. She had got good grades in her first semester.

"We are back with these cuties!" Aiden shouted as all the customers turned their head. Five kittens and five puppies were peeping through their boxes. The delighted customers ran and took out the babies from their boxes and started playing with them. Aiden stood beside Amelia, "This is a good profit making strategy. This place feels like home more nowadays, don't you think so?" Amelia nodded her head while sipping her latte. It was raining outside and the weather was perfect for some enjoyment. Amelia turned the speakers on and the customers started dancing on the tunes. This was the main difference between Doccos and Olivia was that Doccos wasn't lively at all and life thrived at Olivia.

"You got your results?" "Yeah I got them a while ago. I passed with good grades. I think I will drop some classes and opt for better ones. I need to focus at the café and studies simultaneously. I am so tired at times and yesterday the bulletin board had an announcement that we have a fest and only 'couple entries' are allowed. Now, everyone is going around the campus asking for a partner." "Do you plan to go?" "Obviously yes because we are going to perform at the talent show. We need some merits of performing at a school event before the second term starts." "You need two of those, so how do you plan for the next merit." "Let me take part in this one first, I will worry about the next one later. Aiden, do you know a good partner for me?" "Try asking me. I will never refuse. When is the talent show?" "Day after tomorrow. Remember to pick me from the dorm building." Amelia walked to the hearts and drew one and wrote something on it. Aiden, finding it amusing, followed her to the heart tree. Amelia hung it to one string and went inside to take care of her pets. Aiden went and read her note and smiled. It read as,

"**Aiden, take me out on a dance, will you?**"

After an hour of complete chaos and explaining her workers how to handle, feed and where to keep the pets, Amelia walked out of her café. She looked up at the sky to see the stars twinkling beautifully. She loved the night as it helped to hide the expressions on her face. She had an appointment with Ms. Carol and she felt kinda nervous. She took three deep breaths and walked past the heart tree. She paused and retraced her steps back to the tree. Curious whether Aiden had read her note, she searched for it. When she found it, she turned it around. She blushed at his reply,

"I wouldn't dare to dance with any girl except you. I would love some salsa anytime ;)"

It was morning in the dorm and all the girls had classes in the afternoon. "Who are you all going with tomorrow? Jessica, Amelia and Georgia, don't answer cause we all know who it is." Amelia and Georgia giggled at this while Jessica blushed. Caden, the guy who had asked to her first dance at the fresher's party had proposed to her a day before and she had agreed to date him. "Well that leaves me, Fiona, Tanya and Yaniya out." Yaniya stood up. "I have something to confess to you all." Everyone turned to her with excitement in their eyes, anticipating that Yaniya had a secret boyfriend or something. They had seen her blushing from some days before but hadn't forced or compelled her to reveal her secret. "I have a partner to go with and I don't think I will be able to hide this secret any longer." Maria patted her head as an approval that she can speak the name that everyone was waiting for from so long. "I am dating Fiona," Yaniya gulped as she said this. Maria looked shocked at the mention of her twin, dating another girl. She had heard about people being bisexual but never in her most terrifying dreams had she thought that her sister might be affected by this disease. She held her sister's hand and glared at Yaniya, "Stay away from Fiona! I don't want her to be affected by you and your weird company" and she walked away, turning a deaf ear to the others as Yaniya sat down, her head in her hands.

Amelia signaled Jessica, Tanya and Georgia to follow the twins while she started patting Yaniya's back as she continued sobbing. "You should have given us some hints or a heads up. We would have backed you." "Amelia, even you think that being bisexual is a disease? I am human, can't I choose with whom I fall in love and decide my own sexuality? Fiona loves me too. I have been interested in her since a long time but had I known that this would cause a rift between us friends, I would have never confessed to Fiona. She isn't at fault and I wasn't able to control my emotions. I should have been more efficient friend. I had told my parents about me being bisexual and even at home I was continuously mentally harassed by it. That's why I had opted to stay in the dorms even though having my home here. My mother had warned me and my father had threatened to disown me. Finally I had fought with them and earned my own money to take admission here. I worked hard, saved money and gathered myself before coming here. My parents haven't spoken to me in a long time but I don't regret moving out by myself and living as a bisexual but I still hate it that people keep seeing me as someone who has got illness in her brain or something."

Amelia hugged Yaniya, "You are strong and I am proud of you. I am happy that you spoke what was on your mind. You came out clear to your parents. Being bisexual or having any different sexual identity doesn't define you or make you outcasts. This society has been making rules and expecting us to follow them. In the long course of time, people have forgotten to use their hearts but depend on orders that they have to follow. We are not different from the computer codes that we write; both work on commands and there is no automatic stopping to it. We have to pause it ourselves and turn it off. I will talk to Maria and try to persuade her. Fiona may need her support when she comes out of the closet in front of her family. You have one work and that is you don't have to give up. I think it's time for your shift at the laundry shop. I will see you in the evening for dinner in the cafeteria and just focus on your work and

I will try my best to change her mind." Yaniya wiped her tears and muffled a thank you. She walked towards the exit slowly as she soon faded out of sight.

Amelia sighed and called Georgia. Georgia wasn't picking her call and assuming that they were still trying to calm Maria and protect Fiona from her wrath, she hurried to the campus playground searching for her friends. She passed Ashley, who seemed curious to see a worried expression on Amelia's face. She followed her to the class beside library. Amelia saw Maria sitting stiff and not paying any heed to the girls pleading and Fiona, who kept on looking everywhere, maybe searching and waiting for Yaniya. Ashley hid behind the door as Amelia walked inside. Relief flooded on Fiona's face as she saw Amelia walk in. Maria looked at Amelia, with tears in her eyes, "Are you here to persuade me too?" "I am not going to persuade you to allow Fiona and Yaniya to date each other. I am here because I am against it too." Fiona and the others looked shocked and their jaws dropped as Amelia said this. Maria stood up and hugged Amelia. "You are a true friend to me." Amelia patted her back, "But what are your exact reasons to not allow them to be together? I support you as you are my friend but Fiona is also my friend. So when someone asks me why I took your side and not Fiona's, what reason should I give them?"

Maria took a step back, "They are both girls and them being together doesn't make them fit to live in the society. Who will accept them and give them respect in them? Them being together will be considered as a sin in the society and I have to protect my sister in the eyes of the public." "Wait a minute now Maria. So when someone asks me that why I didn't support Fiona, I have to say that I didn't stood by her because I was afraid of society? The same society which doesn't care whether a person lives or dies, the one who judges a person's worth by what brand they wear, the society that gives importance to status more than a person's life? You are against your sister and Yaniya's dating just because of the society. In whatever you said, not once did you say that YOU have any problem with them. Yaniya had disclosed her sexuality to her parents some time back and they didn't support her as they were preoccupied with the society and its rules. Yaniya had to move out and earn her own bread just for the cause that her parents might accept her back as their own daughter. You are doing the same with Fiona. What if one day she moves out and starts living on her own just cause her sister wasn't going to support her for her own happiness? We fall in love with animals, regardless how grown up we are. But while falling in love with a human, why don't we just follow our heart? You might be able to keep Fiona in your control now but do you think that you can do that forever. There is one time in everyone's life when they turn into rebel. If you support her now, she might be with you forever and you both might continue to have a good bond as today or else, she might end up alone without a family despite of having one."

Maria looked at Amelia, finally understanding what she meant. She turned and hugged her sister firmly, "I would support you for my entire life rather than losing you and our bond." Fiona hugged her back as she smiled at Amelia. The others looked at Amelia with the same respect that they had for her since the day they had met. Fiona broke the embrace gently and walked up to Amelia, "I knew you would help us." Amelia smiled, "WE helped you. I wasn't in this alone." The girls beamed at each other and Tanya reminded Maria that she had to apologize to Yaniya. The girls, then walked arm in arm to the dorm unknowingly that

Ashley had heard everything.

Yaniya was being pampered in the dorm at the evening when Amelia had returned from the café. Maria hadn't wasted a single moment and begged Yaniya for forgiveness. Amelia took her nightwear and had a shower. She had visited Ms. Carol again and had continuously transferred $100 to the same number that she transferred her money to, until the sum total was $2,000. 'I need to make money to take care of him. I am grateful that the business is going well or else it would've been a hassle.' She came out, her hair glistering due to water and sat at her table and opened her laptop in order to complete her assignment. She started writing her assignment when a notification popped up on her screen. It was the notification from the campus forum where one could access all the daily news and gossips. Amelia had to keep a check on the forum as it was her way of knowing whether her customers were interested in her café and what other changes were needed to make their time in the café worthwhile.

The first heading that popped on the screen as soon as Amelia clicked open it was:

TEEN BISEXUALS FOUND DATING ON CAMPUS with their friends support. PLAN ON ATTENDING THE FEST TOMORROW AS A COUPLE and officially announcing their relationship.

Amelia chocked on her water and found Yaniya's and Fiona's pictures attached below. The comments below were discouraging. She had just convinced Maria to accept Fiona and Yaniya and now this. When she saw the account that had posted this, @ASHLEY_XOXO, she got up and opened the door with a loud bang. The others got frightened and followed Amelia all the way to Ashley's dorm room. She knocked the door politely and as soon as the door opened up, she pushed the girl and walked inside the room. Ashley was sitting with her legs cross, typing something on her laptop. "Delete the post this instant," Amelia said, as softly as she could. "How can I do so? My post has reached over 43k people and there are about 23k comments that support me. Aww...poor Yaniya and Fiona, they had just started to date but because their friend is an irritating person, they have to suffer the results too. I am starting to feel pity for them after all this disease is incurable and I don't want others to be affected..." and Amelia slapped Ashley before she could say other word. Ashley glared angry at Amelia but shut up as she saw that Amelia was glaring at her with much hate and won't be afraid to slap her once again. Amelia pulled the laptop towards her and deleted the post herself. "What is your password?" Amelia asked Ashley. "You ask as if I would tell you," Ashley scoffed. Amelia titled her head and bit her lip. She started to press some buttons. "Here you go. Your laptop is all safe and sound but I suggest that you check your profile out," saying this Amelia walked out of the room. The others were not able to understand what had happened, but they followed Amelia to the dorm room. Ashley opened her profile but was unable to do so. She tried to search for her profile many times but wasn't able to load it until she realized that Amelia had deleted her profile. She opened her mailbox to check whether she had received the mail to stop the account from deleting and sure enough there was a mail. But when she had to confirm her email id and password, she couldn't do so because Amelia had changed all her passwords and deleted all her social media accounts.

Amelia had just returned to the dorm and she sat on her bed with her laptop. The others saw that she was vigorously typing something. They sat on her both side and saw the post that she was uploading on the school forum. Amelia posted it and went to the bathroom. The others opened the forum and read the post,

Love neither has boundaries nor limitations. Falling in love is the loveliest feeling in the world. You may fall for a person of opposite gender or they may belong to your own gender. I support my friends and I am proud that they had the guts to come forward and tell people their true feelings. I wonder how many such people are there in the campus, that are afraid to come out cause they mind what the society says.

I would like to invite all of our LGBTQ community to reveal their true selves so that we can welcome them and embrace them. It's high time that we start loving everyone and stop labeling others when we know it deep inside that even we, aren't perfect.

Within the next hour, there were 20k likes and 16k messages supporting the post.

Amelia's Diary,

Yaniya and Fiona came out of the closet as they declared their sexuality. Maria had taken this in the wrong way as she thought that SOCIETY wouldn't accept them. Little did she forget that the so called SOCIETY is made up of us, the normal people. If we start changing our thinking process slowly and steadily we will be able to change the laws of society and by changing them, we will be able to spread love again and without conditions this time.

CHAPTER NINE

Chapter 9

"Do you think that people will come?" Jessica asked Tanya nervously who bit her lip as a negative gesture. The girls were already on the fest ground with their partners. Amelia was with Aiden, Georgia with Noah, Jessica with Caden, Yaniya with Fiona, Maria and Tanya were with their classmates as their date. They had a performance within the next 20 minutes. They were going to have a mini concert and their main singer of the day was Tanya. Tanya had a problem while speaking however; it disappeared when she sang which was a miracle in itself.

Amelia was looking around anxiously trying to search for at least one such couple that would put her mind on ease. Aiden smiled at her, held her hand and stroked her hand slowly and lovingly, "Your focus should be on Yaniya and Fiona. You don't need other people to support you when you know that you are right. Look at those two, they are smiling because they have the support of all their close friends and that is their strength. They don't matter if someone supports or doesn't. You should smile and enjoy the present moment. That is all that matters." Amelia looked at Aiden, amusingly and smiled at him.

"Next we have COPINES on the stage. Welcome them with a huge round of applause. But before they arrive, we have a message for them from the audience today." The girls looked at Amelia, "I didn't plan anything and it doesn't have anything to do with me. Don't give me that look" Amelia defended herself. Some people came on the stage and took over the stage, "I am Ben and I am gay." The entire place that was filled with the loud noises suddenly went silent. "This is my boyfriend Clark. The people behind me are also some people that belong to LGBTQ community. We had expected the same reaction that you have given now, when we would announce our relationship to the public. When people ask me what my relation is with Clark, I always say that we are best friends because I am afraid of the criticism that we will face when I say that I am his boyfriend. However, I am not afraid today. You may think that this is a publicity stunt or some kind of drama but, Amelia, we all thank you from the depth of our hearts. Maybe people will still not support us, maybe they will call us names or something or maybe they will shun us endlessly. That won't matter to us now. Yesterday when we read your post, we saw that there are people who will support us and that encouraged us to take this step. Thank you very much. We will be grateful to you for the rest of our lives cause you taught us to find our own voice."

Amelia ran to the stage and hugged Ben as the entire crowd started cheering loudly. The girl ran behind Amelia, with tears in their eyes as they acknowledged Amelia their greatest strength. The night ended with the girls singing songs and all the couples, no matter their sexuality, dancing and flaunting their true selves without worrying about the society and its rules.

Amelia woke up refreshed to see the others hurrying out for their classes and Maria sleeping soundly. Apparently, Maria had fever in the night and was out from the sleeping effects of the pill. Amelia didn't have any classes today as her professor was out of town. She told the others that she would take care of Maria and go around the café area for some time. She got up and tided the room and took a quick shower. 'The room has become too messy these days. Well can't blame anyone, we all were preoccupied with lots of stuff. Let's take the mop now,' Amelia thought to herself as she picked the mop and started mopping the floor. She had just started but saw a medicine bottle under Maria's bed. She bent down and read the label. Amelia called Ms. Carol and spoke with her and noted down certain instructions. She called Dr. Froster, a senior physiologist and Ms. Carol's father. After talking with him and fixing an appointment for the next day, Amelia resumed her work. She had finished with the work when Maria woke up. "Get ready fast! I have checked your temperature and its fine. Let's grab a bite at Olivia and then go shopping. I have to shop some fabrics for the next week." Maria nodded her head and walked into the bathroom as Amelia started to get ready.

"A plain cheese sandwich for me and do you want anything Amelia?" "Plain cheese sandwich? Sasha, give Maria French Toast and pass me a strawberry milkshake." Maria pouted as she looked at Amelia. "I know you are on your periods and plus you have fever. It's better that you eat more and healthy." Maria smiled at Amelia but Amelia noticed the tinge of restlessness in her Maria's eyes. "Maria...there is something that we should talk about. If you don't mind, can we step out for a moment?" Maria signaled in affirmation and the two walked outside to the 'heart tree.'

Amelia didn't waste a moment and took out the medicines that were found under Maria's bed. Maria's eyes widened with fear and nervousness. She started sweating profusely and clenched both her hands. Amelia saw the panic attack and she quickly placed her hand on Maria's right shoulder and held her left hand as she patted Maria. "Take deep breathes with me. One. Two. Three. Four. Five. Six. Seven." Amelia helped Maria to calm down. Once she made sure that Maria had calmed down, she wiped the sweat off her head, "I am sorry Maria. I didn't expect that you will might get a panic attack. But since when have you started taking antidepressants? Why didn't you tell anyone of us? I know one thing for sure Maria, these are not taken under prescription. Would you like to explain me the reasons behind this?"

"Fiona and I are twins and we were brought up with love and care however, Fiona was always favored over me. My parents, friends, my first crush have always preferred her over me. I have always felt like I have been under her shadow. She is prettier than me, she is smarter, she is good with her studies and she is perfect. But me? Look at me. I am a nobody and there is no way I am capable enough to compete with her. I am scared that I might be left alone and everyone would pick her and this is pressurizing me." Amelia frowned. "I may try to understand your situation, but I can't. The person who experiences pain, only that person can know how much it hurts. No one else can ever understand anyone other's pain. However, I want you to stop taking the antidepressants." Maria looked horrified at this, "Amelia, I am able to sleep at night just because I take them. I have been taking them since the last 3 years and I don't think I can let them go." Amelia patted Maria's head, "There is no addiction that can't be overcome. I have scheduled an appointment with a well known physiologist. We can go there tomorrow in the evening." "B...but Amelia, my parents can't know about it! I don't have a financial backing to support me. I can't pay the fees." "No one is asking you to pay anyone. Your treatment is on me. But before that, we need to pull the root cause of this entire problem. You have to confess your insecurities to Fiona tonight. I will be there with you. Not speaking for you but motivating you to speak."

"That's all for your last session Maria. Now get lost from here and I don't want to see you in my clinic anymore," Dr. Froster laughed as Maria smiled back at him. It had been 15 weeks and 30 sessions that helped Maria to believe in herself. She was back on her feet. "I have brought some pancakes. I really wanted to thank you for your time and guidance doctor." "The entire credit goes to Amelia. She sent you to me at the right time. Thank that blessed child for everything. She is an angel with invisible wings." "I am going to thank her too. Today is her birthday and I have made many plans but the biggest one is that Aiden is going to propose her tonight." "Is it the 16th already?" Dr. Froster asked with a frown on his face. "Yes, today's 16th April. We have planned a party so I need to be going now. I will call you later. Thank you." Maria rushed out from the room as Dr. Froster sighed, "Time flies fast."

"Are you all done? I want it to be perfect." "Aiden, she hasn't even read your text yet. Why are you wasting the time on instructing us? Call and check on her first." "Noah, I have called her about ten times. Maybe she is busy with dressing up. She sent all the girls here when they told that we are having a party here. She will be here within a short time." The clocked chimed 9PM. Then it chimed at 10PM. Then at 11PM. The others looked at the teary eyed Aiden. The bouquet of lavenders had bloomed and waiting for the person they were made for. At 12AM, Aiden stood up and kept the bouquet at the counter and walked outside without any other word. The rain decided to accompany him and comforted him the entire night as he walked out.

CHAPTER TEN

Chapter 10

Amelia had left the room that night. Her things were gone. She had withdrawn from the course. Her mobile was switched off. No one had any idea where she was. The guard had told Aiden that she walked out with her suitcase and hired a taxi. That was the last time she was ever seen around the university. Everyone on the campus started an outlook for her. Everything was in utter chaos. Finally, after a fruitless search, the group was sitting in Olivia, drinking cold drinks after a day's searching when Ashley and Kevin walked inside the café. "Seems like your girlfriend-to-be ran from you, Aiden." "Cousin, I already told that Amelia was not a good girl. Now you are wasting your time looking for her when she left you without any hesitations and look at you all!" Ashley pointed at the girls, "Your leader ran away from you. Well, I can't say what she did was wrong according to the fact that she didn't want to be associated with a bunch of losers like you."

Jessica stood up and slapped Ashley without blinking, "Get out." She then turned to the others, "Amelia wouldn't like us looking for her like this. She made us strong enough to be dealt with. She ran on her own. She will come on her own. Don't lose your hope everyone. We should focus on our studies and taking care of each other. If we know our

Amelia, we should believe that she will come back. I had gone through her mails and had seen that she had got an offer from the 'King's' brand. She had signed up for it..." "You've got a delivery!" It was a set of scented candles along with a letter in Amelia's handwriting. It read as:

I will see you soon!

"See, she sent us these. Take these and let's go to our rooms." Aiden nodded as relief flooded all over his face. The past days that were filled with anxiety, sleeplessness and tension were over. 'Firefly, wait till I catch you now and this time, I will cage you with my love.' It became a habit for the next five years. Different gift were delivered to Olivia on the 25th of every month along with short messages like, **eat on time, take care :) , sleep well, I love you all.** Finally the graduation day dawned. Noah had come to the graduation of his girlfriend and had a ring in his pocket. These 5 years with Georgia had made him realize how beautiful it was to fall in love with the right person. Aiden had tagged along with him cause the last 25th, the message that Amelia had sent was **I will meet you soon! It's finally your graduation.** The girls were all getting ready with their stuff. Amelia's influence on them of helping everyone in need had earned the girls quite a name in the university.

"Now the next award goes to the group of COPINES. Give a big round of applause to Jessica, Maria, Fiona, Tanya, Yaniya and Georgia." The girls climbed on the stage and bowed to everyone present. "Professor, can we wait for some more time? We are waiting for Amelia to show up. She has sent us the message that she will be here." "I am afraid that we don't have that much time in our hands." The girls looked at each other and agreed for the ceremony to proceed on. After the awards and collecting their degrees, the girls ran to Noah and Aiden. "Did you see Amelia?"

The boys shook their heads. "She will be here soon. I heard that there was traffic from the airport to the campus. Many people are traveling for the graduation. Let's go to Olivia and wait for her there, shall we?" Aiden suggested.

"Will you marry me?" Noah was on his knee with a diamond ring in his hand and Georgia had already started to cry her lungs out. "Yes!" Noah put the ring on Georgia's finger and took her in his arms and kissed her. The others clapped in union and the entire café congratulated the two. A loud horn came from the outside and the group ran out. A big black car. Dazzling and looking dominating enough. The door opened and a foot stepped out. Long black pencil heel with matching black jeans and a white shirt. The only problem was that the person in these clothes was not Amelia but Ms. Carol. She smiled brightly at the others and walked up to them. "These are Amelia's gifts to you all." "Where is Amelia? When will she be coming back? Is the flight late?" "A....am....Amelia ssss..ss...sss....sent gifts but wwhh..ehhher......where is she?" "Here is her letter to you and congratulations on your graduation. I will be leaving on now."

"Give me the file," Aiden asked irritated by this gesture. He read the papers and his eyes opened wider with each page he flipped. "What does it say?" Yaniya asked Aiden. Aiden cleared his throat, "Amelia has transferred the café under 7 names. Sasha, Jessica, Yaniya, Maria, Fiona, Georgia and Tanya. She transferred the heart tree under my name. What the hell this girl is doing?" Aiden threw the file in anger. He opened his mobile and called on the old name 'Amelia' that he hadn't called in the past 5 years and sure it was still switched off. "Open the letter Aiden. Maybe she has written why she has done this." "Jessica, you read the letter aloud. I don't want to read anything for the time being."

Jessica opened the letter and started reading from it,

You all must've been graduated by now. What a great scene it must've been! Sadly I won't be able to see it. My mother had passed away after giving birth to me and my father always told me that my birth was the reason for her death. He abused me both physically and mentally but God didn't seem satisfied with gifting me so less problems. By the age of 15, I was diagnosed with heart disease. I got a big hole in my heart with got bigger and dangerous with every passing day. I had met Ms. Carol there and I will be eternally grateful to her. My father didn't have funds for my operation and when I got my mother's insurance money, I was already 18 and it was too late. I didn't want to just sit and die one day so I started working.

I earned money and shifted to Hamlington, I found friends for the first time and I was truly happy here. My father, a drunkard, still wanted to leech off his sick daughter and I transferred him money ever week cause he threatened to destroy my life here. After coming here and hearing everyone's problems made me feel that I should solve them as the solution of my problem is far- fetched. My disease had a rare cure and as I am writing this letter a night before my last surgery. I wrote all the notes and prepared all the gifts tonight and had asked Ms. Carol to keep you believing that I was still alive and well.

I feel contented because for the first time in my life, I had people who loved me. Maybe this letter will act as my last words that I wanted to tell everyone. Ms. Carol thank you for being the mother I never had. Tanya, thank you for dressing me every day and smiling like the sun, warm and refreshing. Jessica, thank you for making sure that I was alright. Yaniya, I found comfort in you. I trusted you the most and thank you for being my secret keeper. Maria and Fiona, thank you for making me laugh when I felt broken. Georgia, thank you for the ever-lasting secret late night treats. Noah, thank you for teaching me how to be a warrior.

And lastly, Aiden, I don't know what to write about you. You're the first guy I fell in love with, the one I tried to imagine my future with, the one that made me blush, the one, the one that had my whole heart (excluding the hole in the heart, obviously <3). Thank you Aiden for teaching and showing me how beautiful it is to fall in love. It would be foolish of me to not apologize from running away that night you were going to propose me. I knew about it and if I were alive, my answer would be YES!

Guys, I really don't want any of you to cry after you read this letter because this life has been too hard for me and I need a good rest. I will start once again, in next birth. Let us all meet in the next life too and grow old together. Trees need to shed the autumn leaves so that it can grow the fresh ones again. A firefly brings the light to happiness along with it but soon as the light goes off, it can't help you again. Thanks for being the fireflies to my life.

Till then, goodbye.

Yours lovingly,

Amelia Araste

That day, at Olivia, everyone bawled their eyes out. It would be foolish to tell who cried the most. The next day, the group visited the hospital and spoke with Ms. Carol. She told them where Amelia rested and they went to the grave. Aiden bent down to the grave and touched it, "This is where you have been all the while, huh?" Yaniya walked beside Aiden, "Amelia, we have come here with our letters. We will bury them around you. Make sure that you read all of them." The group dug the soil around the grave and buried their letters with tears in their eyes. "Thank you for begin the firefly to our lives, Amelia." And slowly Aiden mumbled, "I will wait for you in every life, MY FIREFLY."

9 798887 725857

Printed by Libri Plureos GmbH in Hamburg, Germany